Twisted Shorts

By
Andrew Lennon

By
Andrew Lennon

Available on Amazon Kindle and Print

A Life to Waste
Keith
Twisted Shorts – Ten Chilling Short Stories

Copyright © Andrew Lennon 2015

The right of Andrew Lennon to be identified as author of this Work has been asserted by him in accordance the Copyright, Designs and Patents Act 1988.

All rights reserved.
This eBook is copyright material and must not be copied, reproduced, transferred, distributed, leased, licensed or publicly performed or used in any way except as specifically permitted in writing by the publishers, as allowed under the terms and conditions under which it was purchased or as strictly permitted by applicable copyright law. Any unauthorised distribution or use of this text may be a direct infringement or the author's and publisher's rights and those responsible may be liable in law accordingly.

This collection is a work of fiction. Names, characters, businesses, organizations, places, events, and incidents either are the product of the author's imagination or are used fictitiously. Any resemblance to actual persons, living or dead, events, or locales is entirely coincidental.

For more information about the author, please visit
http://lennonslair.blogspot.co.uk/

To Mark

Happy Birthday, Bro. Enjoy

Table of Contents

An Introduction from Michael Bray

Nightmares

Daddy's Girl

Slayer

Externals

Family Man

Tears of a Clown

Time

Devourer

Throw a Punch

The Swings

An Introduction from Michael Bray

Whenever I'm asked to write an introduction or foreword to a book, I find it incredibly humbling that a fellow colleague cares enough to approach me in the first place. Those thoughts are quickly replaced by what the hell I intend to write about!

Nevertheless, when Andrew asked me to write an introduction to the collection you are about to read, I was more than happy to do so. He, like myself, is one of the new breed of authors trying to break through into a business which we clearly love. I feel fortunate to find myself growing alongside such talented individuals, people who I'm sure will become or in some cases are already becoming the go-to names for readers looking for their next favourite writer. It's exciting to be a part of it, and to see people I class as my colleagues and friends gaining the success they deserve makes me feel confident that the genre we write in is in safe hands.

Andrew is one of those writers. I haven't known him personally for too long, although I had seen his work. Like many of my colleagues in the industry, I see in him the thing that links all of us together. The desire to create, to craft stories that will delight, terrify and leave a lasting impression is backed up by one thing which I think separates those who will make it and those wont.

Hard work.

Without hard work, without absolute dedication, none of us stand a chance to make it in this industry. There are definitely two camps. Those who want to write a book, and those who do write books. The latter are the ones who sacrifice to do it. The ones who dedicate themselves to the craft and learning its intricacies, to master the subtle art of language, pacing and storytelling. Even mastering it isn't enough. The drive to take that knowledge and apply it with the fierce determination and desire to be a success, and in turn give something to the reader which is truly memorable is something I definitely see in Andrew. I know from the conversations that we have had recently, during working on a joint anthology called Behind Closed Doors, that he has a feverish desire to succeed. He has all the tools needed to be a huge name in the industry, and I hope this collection is another small step towards that goal.

For those of you who read and love the horror genre for its ability to make the hairs on the back of the neck stand on end, or to make you pull that stray leg back under the covers for fear something might come out of the night and grab you, I would recommend keeping a close eye on Andrew and the works he releases going forward.

I know I'll be watching closely and waiting to see what horrors he produces next.

- **Michael Bray**

Nightmares

I sat in my car, parked on the driveway. I waited, trying to come up with what to say to Tess, because as soon as I walked into the house she would ask me what the doctor had said. I told her I would go to speak to a doctor about my nightmares because we couldn't go on like this.

For weeks, the dreams had been getting worse, affecting her too. My screams, or crying, in the middle of the night would wake her up, and the both of us got more tired and depressed with each sleepless night. I couldn't tell her I didn't go to see the doctor after all. But I had to, so I got out of the car and stood there for a second, staring at the front door. I walked along the path to the house. I felt like throwing up. It shouldn't have been that much of a big deal.

After standing outside my front door for what was felt like a lifetime, I opened it and walked in. "Tess," I shouted. "I'm home."

I went into the kitchen to make myself a cup of tea. Next to the kettle lay a note.

Gone out with Trish and Debra. Be back late, don't wait up. Dinner in microwave. Love you. Tess. xx

Great! It gave me until morning to think of something to tell her about the doctors. If I left for work early enough I'd even have until tomorrow night.

A lot more relaxed, I opened the microwave to see what dinner would be. Shepherd's pie. My stomach rumbled, but it would take two minutes to heat it. I set the timer and then went to get out of my clothes.

It took me about thirty seconds. I threw my shirt and pants next to the washing machine, but kept on my boxers. I refreshed my skin with a blast of deodorant.

PING!

I took the pie out of the microwave. On my way to the living room I got myself a beer out of the fridge as well. I sat in front of the TV, ate and watched *Sports Greatest Mishaps*. It was 10.30pm by the time the program finished and by then I'd had more than enough beer, I counted five bottles. It was time to call it a night since I had a plan to get up early to avoid Tess, before she could ask me the question I couldn't answer.

I went to bed and hoped that I fell asleep before Tess got home.

My sleep was interrupted by a loud noise coming from downstairs. I sat up, listened, and looked around. Tess still wasn't home, evident by her vacated side of the bed. I waited for a moment. I could hear sounds again, not loud this time, it sounded like items being shuffled around in a drawer.

This wasn't Tess coming home.

Someone had broken in.

I jumped out of bed. I ran down the stairs, bare feet muffled by the carpet, and turned the lights on. Broadening my shoulders and sticking out my chest, I paced from room to room. "When I find you in my house, stealing my stuff, I'm going to seriously kick your arse," I shouted.

But there was no one. I checked every room and found nothing. Had it been Tess after all? Maybe she tried to get in the front door and was too drunk. When I opened it, there was nothing. Nobody on the doorstep, no drunken female on the lawn. I glanced down both sides of the empty street, the chilled air making me shiver. Closing the door, I went to the kitchen and got a glass of water, then wandered back to bed.

I glanced at the clock, it was gone midnight. Tess should be home soon. Still wanting to avoid the whole dream conversation, I tried to get to sleep again. Within seconds, the front door opened. High heels clattered around, and from the sound of it she was at the end of a good night. I lay still and closed my eyes, to look asleep when she came in the room.

"Who are you? What are...*get off me!*" Then she screamed

For the second time that night, I leapt out of bed and raced down the stairs, only this time I *knew* there was someone in the house, and they had Tess. The screams didn't stop. They got louder as I approached the bottom of the stairs...only there wasn't a bottom. Every time I got within two steps, more appeared, like an escalator coming up from my ground floor. I carried on, frustration building, trying to land on the carpet that was just beyond reach.

"Fuck this."

I jumped, flew through the air, clearing all the steps and hit the wall next to the front door. I crumpled to the floor, suddenly exhausted. The screaming continued. On the wall in the hallway, I could see two giant shadows fighting and prancing, cast from the kitchen.

I had to get up and help Tess.

I scrambled to my feet and ran to the kitchen, the screaming so loud now, like it was inside my head. As I got to the entrance of the kitchen, the door slammed shut. I pulled the handle down to open the door but it wouldn't budge.

Tess's screams got louder.

I slammed my shoulder repeatedly against it, trying to force my way in. I ran to the other end of the hallway, then sprinted back at the door and braced myself for impact. My shoulder clattered the wooden surface at full pace, and it swung open with a crack. I stumbled into the kitchen, turning as the intruder fled out the back door. I didn't get a good look at him, but Tess hung over his shoulder like a rag doll.

He took her away from me!

I sprinted to the exit, the intruder no more than a dark shadow at the far end of the garden. I ran back into the house, and stood in the entrance hallway. Bewildered, I turned around. Behind me was my front door, which was closed. Tess screamed again, this time it came from upstairs, and I sprinted, taking the stairs two at a time.

I needed to save her.

On the landing, I charged into the bedroom, drenched in sweat, panting, like I'd just run a marathon, and landed smack in the middle of a nightmare. Tess lay strapped to the bed, face down, her screams now muffled by the pillow below. On top of my wife sat the most horrendous thing I've ever seen. It had the rough shape of a man, a head, two arms, two legs. But it's skin looked like it had been turned inside out. Patterns, which I'm sure must have been veins and arteries, crisscrossed all over it like bad stitching. It straddled Tess, finding balance atop of my struggling wife, and shoved her face into the pillow once more. Then, it turned its head and looked at me.

I braced myself, sure this thing would charge me. However, it only stared and smiled, revealing the most brilliantly white teeth I'd ever seen. They were jagged and sharp, like those of a sharks. I was almost mesmerized by them. But then Tess screamed again, breaking the spell.

I had to save her. With a scream, I ran at this *thing.*

I held my arms out and jumped across the bed to grab it. Suddenly, I was flying and landed on a hard surface with a clatter. My chin hurt from the impact of colliding with the kitchen floor.

I didn't have time to question what was going on as the screaming got louder again, this time coming from the living room. I jumped up and took a knife from the cutlery drawer, then ran towards the screaming. When I reached the living room, the screaming ceased.

The figure stood in the centre of the room, waiting for me, smiling. Tess wasn't anywhere near. I gazed at the man in terror. His eyes had shining blue irises surrounded by yellow sclera, instead of pure white. I trembled and wanted to cry, but I couldn't.

I had to be strong for Tess.

"What are you?" I asked

He continued to stare at me, and then smiled that horrible grin again. He had a look that suggested he knew something I didn't. What was it? By now, I was sure it was a dream, but what did it all mean? And why hadn't I woken up yet? This was my fault for not going to the doctors. That's what Tess would tell me. The dreams were going to get worse all the time until I got some proper treatment. As if reading my thoughts, the creature slowly shook his head.

"No?" I asked. "What do you mean, no?"

He continued to shake his head, the smile ever present.

"*Where's Tess?*" I screamed.

He laughed. It almost sounded like a roar and echoed throughout the entire house, shaking it to the very foundations.

"Stop laughing at me!"

The laughter got louder, the creatures belly rose and dropped in sync with the booming sound. Then, the room began to shake. He stood tall and strong, raised his hands above his head, arms stretched out, his fingertips almost touching the ceiling.

"*Stop laughing at me!*"

I charged and tackled him. It surprised me at how easily I took him down. When we hit the floor, I crawled on top of him, pinning him to the carpet. His wide, shining blue eyes gazed at me and he still laughed uncontrollably. I had a full view of the sharp, shining teeth as his laugh bellowed throughout the house. I raised my hand high, ready to stab him with the kitchen knife, but it wasn't there. I put both of my hands around his neck and throttled him.

Still he laughed.

I closed my grip around his throat, squeezing even harder. Then his laughter transformed into a strange gurgling sound, followed by crunching and grinding noises. I tightened my grip still. Dream or no dream, this thing was not going to get me. I held my hands around his throat and enforced my vice-like grip. The struggling and bone grinding noises stopped.

He was dead, I had defeated it, whatever it was. I let go and rolled over onto the soft floor. Surprised, I reached my hand down to feel it. I lay in my bed now, the nightmare over.

The light was still on, and Tess lay in bed next to me. I got up, went to the toilet and had a long drink of water from the tap. I rinsed my face slowly and looked at myself in the mirror. That had been one hell of a dream.

No excuses, first thing in the morning, I would call the doctor. It needed to be sorted out.

I walked back to bed and grinned at Tess. With a few drinks in her, maybe I could get lucky. I slowly slid the quilt off of her and climbed on top, straddling her in a very similar position to the demon in my dream. I leaned over to kiss her neck, she loved that. My shadow blocked most of the light, but the bruise on her neck couldn't be missed. I sat up, looking down at Tess. She stared at me, motionless, her eyes wide and glazed over.

Daddy's Girl

Scott stood at the front door, trying to build the confidence to knock. He wasn't sure how to. What was the protocol? If he knocked too hard would it seem aggressive? But if he knocked too lightly did it show lack of manliness?

Does a father even think that way?

He'd been going out with Jane for a couple of months now. She was the first girl that ever made him think that she could actually be 'the one'.

Tonight is the night he gets to meet her father, the surgeon. Just knowing her father's occupation sent chills down Scott's spine. Every time he thought of a surgeon, he would remember images from a number of horror films. A pale man in a bloodied apron, wearing a surgical mask with a scalpel in his hand while looking over him, lying bound and gagged on the operating table.

OK, come on.
Let's do this

Scott raised his hand. This was it. First impressions mean everything. The door opened and a small man wearing a green cardigan rushed towards him.

"*Arghh*," the man screamed.

Scott jumped backwards in shock, almost falling over.

The man questioned him. "Who the hell are you? You scared the bejesus out of me."

"I'm…um, hi…sir, I'm Scott, Jane's boyfriend."

"Well, nice to meet you, Scott. Even if you did scare me half to death. Now, if you'll excuse me. I must be leaving."

Hmm, well he's not what I expected. More geeky than scary.

The man jumped into the red Porsche that was parked on the driveway. The engine roared to life and he drove away.

"Scott?" Jane stood in the doorway.

"Oh, hey." Scott responded, slightly flustered. "How's it goin'?"

"What are you doing? Come in."

Scott entered the house and immediately knew it was bigger than any house he'd ever been in. Vast rooms, high walls, arching staircases. The only thing he could think of to compare it was the millionaire's house from the move *Annie.* He had never felt so inadequate. Jane had never said she lived in a mansion. She'd been to Scott's house countless times. His 'two up two down' felt like a cardboard box now in comparison to this.

"So do you, like, rent a room here or something? Or is this whole place yours?" Scott asked.

"Rent a room?" Jane laughed. "Don't be silly, Scott. This is our home. I suppose it is a bit much when it's only me and Daddy living here, but this house gives him room for his library and his office and stuff."

"How the other half live, eh?"

"What?"

"Oh, nothing. I just didn't realise you lived in a mansion."

"Well, does it matter?"

"No no, it's just…I feel….like a peasant." Scott laughed nervously.

"Oh, don't be silly! Besides, you know I'm not like that. And Daddy isn't either."

"OK, cool. Sorry, I just thought –"

"–don't be silly. Come on in, I want you to meet Daddy."

"I think I just met him," Scott said. "In fact, I think I nearly gave him a heart attack."

"Daddy? Heart attack? Don't be silly. I've never seen him shocked by anything in his life."

"He was coming out just as I was knocking at the door. He just left in his Porsche."

"Porsche?"

"Yeah. He was rushing out. We scared each other and then he took off in that Porsche."

"That's not Daddy!" Jane laughed. "That was Maurice."

"Maurice?"

"Yeah. He works for Daddy. Like his personal assistant or something."

The fear rushed back into Scott's bones after the relief of seeing that funny little man in the green cardigan. Now, he had to go through the whole ordeal again. Jane took his hand and led him through a large double doorway.

Inside stood a very tall, slim man. His hands held straight at his side.

He smiled as Jane and Scott approached. "Jane." He nodded as he greeted her. "And you must be –"

"– Scott", he interrupted. Scott rushed forward to shake the man's hand. "Hi, yes sir. I'm Scott. Really pleased to meet you."

"Scott, this is Daddy," Jane introduced.

"Or you can call me Dr Harrison." He smiled.

"Yes, um…Dr Harrison. Nice to meet you." Words stumbled out of Scott's mouth.

"Likewise." The doctor said.

"Right OK, now you've met, we have to get going." Jane said.

"Yeah. It was nice to meet you, Dr Harrison."

"Have fun."

The doctor stood in the same spot and smiled as Jane and Scott left. He didn't wave. He just kept his hands by his sides.

While driving in his rusted old Ford Fiesta, Scott started to feel more pathetic. He looked at Jane. She looked like a princess. Now, he found out that she actually lived like a princess as well.

And here she was with him.

The pauper.

"Jane. Does it bother you?" Scott asked "You know, that I'm not rich?"

"Don't be so bloody stupid! I'm insulted that you think I'm that shallow, Scott."

She had a point. She had never said anything to Scott about her wealth. Or about his lack of it. Money had never been an issue before so he shouldn't make it one now.

Besides, he knew that her dad was a surgeon. He should have known that she was going to be rich.

Why was is a big deal now?

"You're right. I'm sorry," Scott said.

"It's fine."

"Your dad does scare me a bit though. I was so relieved when I met that little guy in green and then it turns out that your dad really is the big scary surgeon after all."

"Oh, don't be silly. There is nothing scary about Daddy. And besides, as long as you're good to me then you have nothing to worry about. I'm a daddy's girl you know. And he'll do anything to protect me."

"What do you mean?" Scott asked. "That sounded like a threat. Did he tell you to say that?"

"Well, he *is* a surgeon. You know what he could do to you."

"*What!*"

Jane laughed. "Don't be silly. I'm teasing you. Daddy is harmless. And regardless of what your stupid movies and fears tell you, surgeons *save* lives, dummy. They don't take them."

"Yeah, yeah," Scott laughed. "Well, he's still creepy."

Jane gave him a playful punch on the arm.

****

Driving home after their date night, Jane and Scott played the stereotypical young couple in love. They laughed. They giggled. The groped at each other, even while Scott was driving. Scott had a couple of drinks and he was feeling a little bit over confident.

"Have you ever thought about giving head while I'm driving?"

Jane spat her drink out as she laughed with the shock. Her orange Bacardi Breezer dripped down the passenger window.

"You, sir, are seriously mistaken if you think I'm doing something like *that* in a car! I'm a lady."

"Oh, yeah," Scott laughed. "Lady of the manor. Daddy's girl."

"Yeah, and don't you forget it." Jane laughed.

Her hand crept up Scott's thigh. She cupped as she reached his crotch. She could feel him rising from beneath his jeans.

"There is something else I could do though," she whispered.

Jane unbuckled her seatbelt and started to pull his zipper down. Scott could feel himself hardening. He looked down to see if this was actually happening. He'd never felt so horny. He stared at Jane's hand, waiting for it to creep into his fly.

Suddenly the sound of a car horn caught his attention.

He looked up to see a bright white light.

The impact came before Scott had time to react. He jolted forward and smacked his face on the steering wheel.

Jane flew through the windscreen.

Dazed and confused, Scott looked up. Everything was a blur. He tried to focus but all he could see was red.

The windscreen was bright red.

He passed out.

****

The car that Scott crashed into was empty besides from the driver. He walked away relatively untouched. Just a few bruises here and there, as did Scott. Jane died almost instantly. If being thrown through the windscreen didn't do the job then the impact of the road when she hit it certainly did. Her face was so badly mutilated from the glass that her father barely recognised her.

He had never felt so helpless. Dr Harrison had dedicated his whole life to surgery. He had always pushed himself to be the best he could be. Now, when his own daughter was lying on the table in front of him, there was nothing he could do. He just had to look at the messy remains from a car crash.

Jane's mother had died when Jane was three. She'd been diagnosed with cancer shortly before Jane's birthday.

The following two years were spent back and forth to chemotherapy sessions and doctor visits. Jane spent most of that time with child carers and a nanny. When the time came and Mrs Harrison lost her battle with cancer, Dr Harrison vowed that Jane would spend no more time under the care of other people. He would always be there whenever she needed him. She had lost her mother. She didn't need to lose a father as well.

She was going to be daddy's girl.

Having been so successful in earlier years, Dr Harrison was able to take a year off following his wife's death. When Jane finally started school, Dr Harrison started up surgery again, but only during school hours. He insisted that he would not spend any time away in which his daughter may need him. He appointed Maurice as his personal assistant and Maurice dealt with all of his bookings to ensure that there would be no conflicts or crossovers.

As Jane grew older, she needed her father less and less, such is the way of a teenager. However, he still insisted that he would only work during her school hours, just because she didn't need him all the time didn't mean that he wouldn't be there all the time.

If she needed him, he wanted to be available.

He would do anything for daddy's girl.

****

Scott tried to attend Jane's funeral, but Dr Harrison's security staff wouldn't let him get near. The doctor merely glanced up to look at the commotion that was being caused and then he looked back down at his daughter's grave.

The report from the crash had shown that Scott had high levels of alcohol in his system. Was that entirely to blame for the crash? Perhaps not. Maybe it was due to the distraction while he was driving. But it didn't matter. He had been drinking. If he hadn't then maybe his reactions would've been better and he would have swerved out of the way of the oncoming car.

Maybe if he hadn't been drinking he wouldn't have talked Jane into doing what she was doing and then he would never have been distracted in the first place. All that mattered was at the time of the crash, Scott was drunk. He blamed himself for the crash entirely.

And so did everybody else.

The law were yet to decide. *Innocent until proven guilty.*

With the impending court dates imminent, Scott started to spend his days sitting on a bar stool. He would sit alone, running the accident over in his head, ignoring anyone that talked to him. Apart from the barman. He would talk to him to order his beer and then stay silent again until he needed a refill. He would stay there until the bar closed or most times until he was too drunk to hold himself up.

Then the kind staff of the bar would escort him outside and show him the most comfortable wall to lean up against. He'd lost track of the amount of times he woke in the drunk tank at the local police station. Enough so that he was on a first name basis with most of the officers there.

He was fined regularly for his stays in the drunk tank, but it didn't bother him too much, even with the court dates pending. Surprisingly, when you only spend money on alcohol and the bare minimum of food to survive, it lasts longer than you would think. Having been signed off work with clinical depression and lying on almost every medical claim form he could, Scott had quite a considerable income through various benefits and disability allowances. He would never have enough to buy a mansion like Doctor Daddy, but hopefully he would have enough to see him through to an early grave.

Rather the grave than a prison cell.

Friends and family had visited Scott and tried to talk him into getting his life back together. They tried the approach of telling him that this isn't what Jane would have wanted. When that didn't work they tried the harsh approach of telling him that it was drink that killed her in the first place and ruined his life, so why would he spend so much time with it? Nothing worked. Scott ignored everyone. He had decided what he was going to do with his life now and that was to drink until his body gave up on him.

Then it was all over, hopefully before prison came a knocking.

Perhaps in the afterlife he would meet Jane again.

They had only been together a few months, but Scott was so sure that Jane was the one. Having her ripped from his life in the way she was just made those feelings stronger. She was his only chance of happiness and it was taken away from him. Or he destroyed that chance. It didn't matter. There would never be another one so there was no point in trying.

****

"Beer," Scott ordered.

The barman said nothing back. He just carried on his normal ritual of refilling Scott's glass and taking his money. Scott, realising his court date was tomorrow, didn't care. All hope was gone.

A small man entered the bar. Scott could see him out the corner of his eye but he didn't pay much attention to him. The man cautiously approached Scott and tapped him on the shoulder.

"Scott?" the man asked.

Scott didn't reply. He didn't even turn around, he just carried on drinking his drink.

"Excuse me, Scott," the man spoke again.

"Do I know you?" Scott asked without turning.

"Yes, yes we have met once before. My name is Maurice. I work for –"

"–Dr Harrison." Scott turned around suddenly interested.

"Yes, Dr Harrison."

"So, what do you want? I thought the doctor wanted me dead, surely he wouldn't send you for that? No offence, *mate*, but I don't think you could take me."

"No, no," Maurice laughed. "Dr Harrison would like the pleasure of your company for dinner."

"No." Scott turned back around.

"He said you would say that, but he also said that if you really wanted forgiveness for Jane's death then you would reconsider."

Is this what I need? Would having dinner with that man finally let me get on with my life? Perhaps if he can forgive me. Perhaps it would look better in court. Then I can learn to forgive myself?

"When?" Scott asked.

"Well…" Maurice paused for a moment. "Now."

"Now?"

"Yes. I'm afraid that the doctor has to leave on business tomorrow so it would have to be today."

"Well, can I at least go home and change?"

"No need for that, I assure you. The doctor does not care about your appearance. He just wants your company for dinner."

"Right then." Scott downed his beer and belched. "Let's go, Maurice."

****

After the short drive in the Porsche that Scott extremely enjoyed, they arrived at Dr Harrison's house.

Jane's house.

It looked smaller than he recalled. Maybe Jane's death had sucked the life from it. Maurice led the way and opened the front door. Scott followed. Dr Harrison was waiting when they entered. He was just as Scott remembered him - stood straight and tall with his hands by his sides.

"Dr Harrison…" Scott started.

"Scott, thank you for coming. Please come this way. Thank you, Maurice."

The doctor led Scott to the dining room where a roast dinner was already laid. They both sat at opposite ends of the table. "Please, eat," the doctor said.

"Um, OK. Thanks."

Scott started to eat. The food tasted good. It was the best meal he'd had in a long time.

"Scott, my reason for bringing you here is –"

"– You want to know what happened," Scott interrupted.

"Well, I think I know what happened. You were driving drunk and you killed my daughter."

Scott almost choked on his food.

"You took her from me, Scott. And now…" The doctor paused. "Well, now those drugs in your food will be kicking in and you'll pass out at any minute."

"What the hell?" Scott leapt from his seat and ran to the door. He made it far enough to reach the door handle and then flopped onto the floor, unconscious.

****

Scott opened his eyes.

Everything was blurry. He tried to rub his eyes, but his hands where strapped down. He couldn't move them, he tried but they wouldn't budge. His feet were the same. As he looked around, his vision began to clear.

He was in an empty room. He could now see that he was tied to some form of bed. Above him was a hanging light. Around the room there was nothing else apart from brick walls. He could hear footsteps.

A door opened and Dr Harrison entered. He walked slowly until he was stood at Scott's head. He turned on the light which blurred Scott's vision again. All Scott could see was the light and the shadow of the doctor's head.

"Nice to see you're finally awake, Scott. You were out for longer than I expected. I suppose we have the alcohol to thank for that.

Seems to be a common thing with you, doesn't it."

"Dr Harrison, sir, please...I...."

"Shut up, you little shit." The doctor snapped. "You took her away from me. She was the only thing I had in my life. She was daddy's girl and you took her."

"I didn't mean..."

"You didn't mean what? To drink and drive! It's not done by *accident*. You made a conscious decision that night to drive when you shouldn't have. Because of that, my daughter is dead!"

"I'm sorry," Scott cried, tears ran down the side of his face. His eyes were now blurring again and he struggled to see with the light shining in them.

"The thing is, Scott, this has been torture for me. You see, Jane was my life. My whole world revolved around her. Since you took her, every day has been torture. Every single day. Then I got to thinking."

"Please," Scott cried.

"*Listen to what I have to say!*" The doctor roared. "I got to thinking. Why am I torturing myself? When really I should be torturing you."

"No. please."

"Oh come on, you don't even know what I'm going to do yet."

"Please."

"You see, Scott, I like to do research. I don't like doing anything half-arsed so I really put the effort in. I thought; if I'm going to torture you, then I want it to be something really special, you know."

"Dr Harrison, listen…"

"Scott, if you don't shut up I will go and get my scalpel and then I will cut your tongue off."

Scott fell silent. He thought for a moment. If the doctor was talking about going to get his tools, then that meant he didn't have them here with him. Perhaps he was just trying to scare him. That was the real torture. All he had to do was show that he was sorry – really sorry – and then the doctor would let him go.

"You see, Scott. As I said. I like to do research. So I did a lot of research on torture. I wanted something really unique. You know, because my Jane, my daddy's girl, she really was unique. You don't know just how special she was."

The doctor picked something up and held it in front of Scott's face. Scott couldn't make out exactly what it was through his blurred vision. It looked like something metal. His heart rate increased. *This is it*, he thought. *I'm going to die right now*.

"Have you ever heard of The Pear of Anguish, Scott?"

Scott shook his head, too scared to speak.

"It's also known as The Choke Pear. Apparently in the early 1800's some robbers used to use these as a gag. You see, it's pear like shape made it easy for them to place in their victim's mouth. Then, as they turned this key, the pear would begin to open out from all sides, a bit like a flower.

The metal sides would widen and it would choke the victim."

Scott's eyes widened.

"Oh, don't worry I'm not doing that. What interested me more? Did you know that around the 1600's when these devices are thought to have first been invented, they would actually be placed in the vagina or anus of a torture victim? You would slide the closed pear into the anus. Then turn the long key. When the sides opened up it would internally mutilate the victim." The doctor laughed. "Now that does sound like a particularly painful experience doesn't it?"

"Please don't," Scott whimpered.

"No. You see. This was used in the 1600's right through to the 1900's. This torture, while impressive, has been used for hundreds of years. That is not nearly unique enough. Not special enough for my daughter's killer."

Scott began to shake his head from side to side. He tried again to free him arms but there was no use. They wouldn't move.

"I wouldn't struggle too much, Scott. You'll do yourself damage."

Dr Harrison walked to the other side of the room, behind Scott's head, and placed the pear on a table. From there he retrieved another instrument and brought it back to show Scott. It was a copper bowl.

"Have you seen this? The pottery bowl. You ever heard of that one, Scott?"

Scott shook his head.

"This one was another of my favourites. The origins of this aren't certain, but one account recorded was during the Dutch Revolt. Apparently, one of the allies of William the Silent would use this to torture prisoners. It's really quite clever when you think about it. He would take some diseased and starving rats and place them in this pottery bowl. He would then set the bowl open side down on the naked body of the prisoner. When hot charcoal was placed on the bowl, the rats would try and escape from the heat. They couldn't get out of the bowl so there was only one way they could go. They would gnaw their way through the victim. Eating right though the stomach."

The doctor laughed and placed the bowl on Scott's stomach. "Doesn't that one sound special?" Dr Harrison asked.

Scott's bladder let loose. He could feel his urine trickling along his leg. He began to cry again.

"Oh, Scott. Look at what you've done now." He removed the bowl. "Don't worry I'm not doing that anyway. You see I told you daddy's girl was special, she was unique. You don't really think I would do something that had been done before do you? Well *do you?*"

Scott shook his head.

"No. I wanted something that was one of a kind. I decided that I would put my skills to use. I am a surgeon after all.

You can't feel it because of the anaesthetic I gave you, but if you look down to your stomach, you should be able to see some new additions. This is why I didn't restrict your head, you see."

Scott's chest was strapped down so he couldn't sit, but he was able to lift his head to see the skin on his stomach stretched and raised in several places. It looked like there were golf balls under his skin. He panicked and tried to struggle free.

"Like I said, Scott, I wouldn't struggle. You'll do yourself damage. The balls I have placed under your skin are very fragile. Have you ever broken a Christmas bauble? I'm sure you have. Well anyway, those balls in your stomach are made of a very thin glass. It is as fragile as a Christmas bauble. Here, listen."

The doctor pressed gently on one of the balls. Scott heard a slight crack.

"*Please…stop!*" Scott screamed "*Help! Someone!*"

"Honestly, Scott. Do you really think I'm stupid enough to bring you where anyone could hear you scream? *Please*. Anyway, you don't even know what's in these balls yet."

"W…w…what's in them?"

The doctor stood over Scott and held a glass ball in his hand. He showed it to Scott. Inside there were some kind of bugs. Scott turned his head to the side and vomited.

Were those bugs really inside him? Or was this another sick story the doctor was using to torture him.

"What the hell are they?" Scott asked.

"They are called Dermestids. Have you heard of them?"

"N…n…no."

"Hmm…they're also known as Flesh Eating Beetles."

"What the fuck! *Get them out*. Please, I'm sorry!"

"Now now, Scott. Remember, if you struggle, you may crack that glass. You see I thought that these little guys were pretty special. Did you know that sometimes they're used in crime scene investigations? It's true. These little fellas eat away all of the flesh and they leave a perfectly clean bone, thus not affecting any marks that may help to diagnose the cause of death. Cool, hey."

Scott's bladder released again. This time his bowels emptied as well.

"Oh, God. Scott, that's fucking disgusting! I really don't know what Jane saw in you. Anyway, besides CSI, did you know that these little beetles are also used in taxidermy? Basically, they pick a cadaver clean. This way they don't have to use harsh chemicals that can damage the bones. So, I'm sure you can see just how efficient these beetles are."

"Please, Dr Harrison. Don't kill me. I didn't…"

"Oh, I'm not going to kill you, Scott. I'm not a murderer. You see. I have been watching you for a long time, ever since you decided to get drunk and take my daughter's life. From then, I have watched you over and over again. You like to get drunk with an aim to destroy your life. You want an early death, is that it?"

"Please, no."

"I have seen you slowly killing yourself every day. Using the very poison that took my girl! So no. I am not a murderer, Scott. I am not going to kill you. You've been trying so hard to do it yourself I thought I would just speed up the process for you."

Dr Harrison pulled a large leather strap from underneath the bed. He pulled it over Scott's stomach and strapped it on either side of the bed. It lay perfectly across each of the embedded balls.

"Now, Scott. When you decide that your time has come, all you have to do is struggle. Natural struggling will force the body to tense and push the stomach out. With this belt, the slightest push will be enough to break those glass balls and then these little fellas can enjoy their dinner."

"Please!" Scott screamed. "Just let me go!"

"I'd like to say it was nice knowing you, Scott. But it wasn't. I wouldn't hold on too long by the way. The anaesthetic I gave you will wear off in the next hour or so. When that happens you're going to feel every single thing those beetles do. Good riddance, Scott."

The doctor turned off the overhead light and started to walk out the room.

"You can't do this!" Scott screamed as the doctor closed the door. "*Hhhheeeellllpppp!*"

Scott screamed as loud as he could. He tried to sit up to remove the belt.

He heard the cracking.

It sounded like someone walking on glass.

"Oh, shit."

Slayer

"Come on, keep up!" Russell shouted.

Gregg tried to run faster but he struggled to keep up with his friend. He was short and overweight for his age. He hated when Russell turned everything into a race. It was the same result every time. Russell would sprint away laughing and shouted for Gregg to keep up. Gregg would fall further and further behind until he was breathless and bright red in the face.

Russell turned to see that Gregg had fallen way back. He stopped for a moment, beckoning him to run faster. Gregg stopped running and gave him the finger, then he sat down. Russell jogged over and sat next to him.

Russell was tall and slim, he was very athletic. He was in the rugby team, the basketball team and the athletics squad. Gregg, however, liked to sit at home and play on his Xbox.

Gregg beat Russell every time when they played *Left 4 Dead*, however, Russell beat Gregg overall in general day to day life. Russell was a hit with the ladies, Gregg never had any. Russell was always surrounded with friends, Gregg had Russell and that was pretty much it. But Russell liked Gregg, yes, he had a lot of friends but none of them were genuine like Gregg. He knew that he could always rely on him to be up front and honest with him.

"Why do you always have to run everywhere?" Gregg panted.

"Because it's fun," Russell replied. "Besides, let's be honest, it's not gonna do you any harm."

"Fuck you."

"Haha, woah there big guy, less of the hostility."

"Well, don't start giving me exercise speeches."

"OK, fine. Come on, if we don't get home soon we're not going to have time to watch it."

"Fine, but I'm not running."

Gregg straightened up and then both of the boys continued to walk along the road.

They wanted to get back to Russell's house in time to watch the Director's Cut of *Zombie Slayer 4*. It had become a bit of a ritual for the boys. Every Saturday, then would go to Russell's and watch a horror movie. They were going through a bit of a zombie phase right now so they were methodically going through the entire *Zombie Slayer* series.

The walk from the video shop was about thirty minutes. It would be a five minute run to Russell, but after a little bit of moaning from Gregg, the run was always cut short seconds after it started.

Strolling along, they talked about how cool the movie was going to be. This one apparently had more blood spatter than any of the others and Gregg heard rumours that there was one bit where you see one of the zombies get his head completely crushed by some big muscle guy, with his bare hands!

"OK, well, whether you want to run or not, you have to now, man," Russell said.

They'd reached the main road across from Russell's house. Three lanes wide and constantly filled with speeding traffic, it was commonly joked between kids that crossing this road was like playing a life-size game of *Frogger*.

"Yeah, I know, I know." Gregg sighed.

"Well, I don't wanna get flattened, do you?" Russell joked.

"Shut up."

"Oh, come on!" Russell laughed.

He ran out into the road, still looking at Gregg as he did so.

Out of nowhere, Russell was smashed by a lorry driving at 60mph. Russell's body flew through the air, limp as a rag doll. Gregg stood dumfounded, his mouth gaped open as he watched his friend land with a sickening, soggy splat on the road. The lorry driver braked but the momentum of the lorry kept it moving. Russell's body was yanked back up by one of the wheels. It was dragged under the lorry, the flesh burning away as it pulled along at high speed.

Eventually the lorry stopped. Gregg could see nothing of his friend. All that was visible to him was the crimson streak where he had been scraped along the road. The rest of him was under the lorry, somewhere.

For weeks after Russell's death, Gregg cried himself to sleep.

He couldn't get the horrific image of his friend being dragged across the road out of his mind. In reality, it had been a blur, he'd disappeared underneath the lorry so fast. In Gregg's memory he could see Russell being pulled along, his head sticking out from the wheel arch, screaming for help. The thoughts were always the same.

And I just stood and watched him die.

But there was nothing he could do. If he tried to sleep, he dreamed about it. So he just sat and cried, and eventually sleep took him into his own little slice of death.

The healing process was delayed more due to the fact that Russell was still yet to have a funeral. Gregg couldn't understand why it was taking so long. He wanted to say goodbye to his friend. He was told that it was because the coroner was having to do a lot of work on Russell to make him "presentable".

He knew that was a load of crap because there was almost nothing of Russell left, from what he had seen. He was also told that it was delayed because the police were investigating the cause of death. Again, he thought that was rubbish because cause of death was blatantly obvious. "Flattened by a lorry," as Russell had said. Unless of course the driver had been drinking or something? Perhaps that could delay it a bit, Gregg didn't know and he didn't care. He just wanted them to hurry up so he could say goodbye.

"Gregg, come and get your dinner!" He heard his mum call.

"Coming!"

Gregg slid himself out of bed and made his way downstairs. As he was passing the phone, it began to ring.

"Hello," Gregg answered.

"Where the hell are you?"

"I'm sorry, what?"

"Where are you?"

"Who is this?"

"What do you mean, who is this? It's Russell you dildo!"

"What?" Gregg asked, a lump in his throat. Tears were filling his eyes.

"I said, it's Russell. Where the hell are you?"

"Fuck you," Gregg slammed the phone down.

When he walked into the kitchen his mum could see the tears in his eyes. She could see that his face was flushed red with anger. "What's the matter?" she asked.

"It's nothing, Mum. Just some prank caller." He sat and ate his dinner in silence. Then he went back to bed.

Later that night the phone rang again. Gregg's mum answered.

"Gregg! It's for you!"

Who the hell is calling for me? "OK, I'm coming!"

He took the phone from his mum and put it to his ear. Before he was able to speak, a voice cut him off. "Where are you?"

Gregg, now grinding his teeth asked, "What did you say?"

"Come on, man! *Zombie Slayer*, remember?"

The breath ran away from Gregg. Nobody else knew of their plans to watch that movie. It was *their* thing.

"R...r...Russell?" he asked

"Yes, Russell! Who the fuck you think it's gonna be, Batman?"

"But...but you...."

"But nothing, come on, man. I've been waiting for you all day to watch this movie. Saturday is horror day, remember."

"Yeah, I remember. I'll be there soon."

Gregg hung up the phone and in a trance like state, he walked to his bedroom to get dressed.

When Gregg left, he told his mum that he was going to Russell's house. His mum didn't question him. She thought that maybe he wanted to go and see how Russell's parents were. The boys spent a lot of time at each other's houses so it was only natural that over time they became friendly with the parents as well.

Gregg thought about running, just so that he could get there quicker, to see if it was actually Russell who called, or if he'd just gone crazy.

But then he decided that if it was Russell, if he really was there, he would get a kick at the thought of Gregg running over. So he chose to walk instead.

Night crept up on him as he made his way to Russell's house. He hadn't realised just how late it had gotten. When he arrived, the house was in darkness. A sense of unease rose in him. He paused for a moment and questioned whether he should be here or not. He knocked on the door.

The door opened, someone stood in the doorway, but it was dark. Gregg couldn't make out who it was.

"You coming in or not?"

"R...R...Russell?" Gregg asked.

"Yeah, of course Russell, what's with you lately?"

Gregg entered the house. Russell led him through the hallway and up the stairs, towards his bedroom. It was so dark with all the lights off. Gregg could just about see where he was going from the moonlight shining through the window from the early night sky.

When they entered Russell's room, Gregg took it upon himself to turn the light on.

The thing that stood in front of him almost made Gregg puke.

Half of Russell's face was gone. It had been scraped away. There wasn't even any facial structure left from his skull.

Just a large, pulpy hole. His arm was so badly broken that it was bending the wrong way. His hip was protruding through his skin and one of his feet looked as though it was purely hanging on by the ripped tendons.

"Holy shit, Russell."

"What?" Russell asked.

"Look at you, you're.....you're dead." Gregg whimpered.

"Yeah, so. You can't say you're surprised. You watched me die."

"But how are you?" He stuttered. "How are you.....here?"

"Fucked if I know," Russell laughed, "but I *am* here, so may as well make the most of it."

"B…b…but…"

"Oh, shut up! B…b…but, that's all you've said. We gonna watch *Zombie Slayer 4* or not?"

Gregg didn't know what to say, he was too shocked to think, let alone speak. He sat himself down on Russell's bed ready to watch the film.

Russell fumbled around for a bit with the tape in his one good hand. "Um, fancy giving me a hand here, buddy?" He joked.

"Oh, um…yeah sure."

Gregg put the tape in and the sat next to Russell on the bed. The movie started.

They sat in silence as the movie played. Gregg didn't notice what was happening, since he was too distracted at the thought of his dead friend sitting next to him.

He carried on looking at him and turned away when Russell noticed. He knew that Russell could see him staring, but what did he expect? The kid was dead for God's sake.

Gregg tried to keep his eyes fixed on the TV now. He already felt uncomfortable as it was, without being caught staring. Russell leaned over to him and put what was left of his mouth on Gregg's neck. Gregg fell off the bed.

"What the fuck are you doing?" He shouted.

"Eating, I'm a zombie, remember?" Russell laughed.

"Argh, what the fuck, no, no, no, no…" Gregg started to cry.

"I'm joking, Gregg. Calm down for Christ sake. Just thought I'd lighten the mood a bit."

"Umm, yeah…very funny," Gregg replied. "I'm gonna go take a piss."

"Oh, come on, you scared of the zombie? Russell chuckled.

"Shut up, dickhead."

Gregg stormed out of the room. It was so dark, he struggled to see where he was going. He felt his way to the bathroom. He eventually found the door handle and opened the door. When he turned on the light, he screamed. The bathroom was painted red.

Russell's parents were lying in the bath tub, severed into bloody pieces.

"What's the matter? I heard screaming," Russell asked from behind.

Gregg shivered with fear.

"Your parents. What did you do to them?" He whispered.

"Oh, they carried on screaming every time they looked at me. It was pissing me off. So I shut them up." Russell said this so casually that Gregg felt a wave of terror seep through him.

"How could you do that to your own……."

"I told you," Russell interrupted. "They were pissing me off, and now you're starting to piss me off as well."

Gregg froze in fear. He stared at the look of evil in Russell's eyes.

"That look," Russell said "That's the look you had on your face when you watched me die."

"I…I…didn't," Gregg mumbled. "I couldn't…"

"I'm going to kill you, Gregg. Hahaha. I'm going to cut your face off so it looks like mine!"

Russell charged towards Gregg. The foot that had been barely hanging on dropped off and he fell to the side. Gregg took this opportunity and ran past him and down the stairs. He headed for the front door.

It was locked.

In a panic, he repeatedly tried to open the door, over and over again. When he turned around Russell had already made his way down the stairs. Gregg ran to the kitchen and tried the back door.

"That's locked as well," Russell called.

He charged at Gregg again.

He was unbelievably agile considering he only had one foot!

Gregg grabbed one of the pans hanging above the kitchen counter and swung it at Russell's face. The edge of the pan slipped into the hole on the side of his face, it took more of the skin away as the swing followed through.

Russell fell to the ground

Gregg had tears streaming down his face. He stood over his friend. "I'm sorry, Russell," he cried, "but I have to. You're not you."

Russell lay on his back, his one eye staring up at his old friend. A horrible gurgling sound was coming from somewhere in his throat. His half lip shaped into a half smile.

"It's OK," Russell whispered. "Gregg, the zombie slayer." He giggled.

Gregg brought the pan down on his friends head again, and again, and again. Until there was nothing but a bloody mess on the floor.

It was a long walk home.

Gregg cried the whole way. When he walked through the front door he was met by his mum. "Oh…..my…..God! What is that all over you?" she screamed.

"This? Oh….it's Russell."

The Externals

I have been staying in this hotel for two days now. I thought I had a chance to escape them. I know now that I was mistaken. I feel them around me. As I sit on this bed and type, I can feel their eyes watching me.

The first sign was subtle; I didn't connect it to them at the time. I kissed my wife and children goodbye and left my house at seven o'clock on Monday morning. I think, even then, I knew that it might be our final goodbye. Too afraid to close my eyes, I hardly slept the night before. I knew that if I did, they would move closer. I was awake with worry.

You can't see them, but they like to watch us, and they like to play with things. They play with us to see how we will react. They see us more as play things than play mates. That was why my sat nav wouldn't turn on when I got in my car. They had tampered with it, played with it. It was another part of their game. They didn't want me to leave; they wanted me to stay with them.

I turned on the navigation system of my mobile phone and used that instead. I made the journey. But they had made the journey also. They are here with me, still.

I am working on an audit with a client this week, so I was going to drive straight to the office, and check in at the hotel later that night. When I turned on the car radio, it was fuzzy. Under the static I could hear giggling, I am sure of it. I changed the channel to hear the traffic news. Traffic was at a standstill on the motorway I needed to take. I should have seen this as another attempt to keep me from going away but I didn't take notice, and chose another route, driving on country lanes for an extra thirty minutes to reach my client's office.

I was so busy setting everything up that the day seemed to fly by. I left the office early so I could check into the hotel. A fifteen minute drive away, the hotel is quite pleasant, a lovely rustic affair. I'm sure it has beautiful views of lakes and woodlands. I have stayed here before, but never seen them, as it is always dark when I am here.

After checking in I make my way to my room on the lower ground floor. I walk away from the reception desk and around a corner leading behind the kitchen entrance. There, I am faced with double doors that are security locked. I unlock them with my key card and walk down the corridor. It is dark, but lights turn on as I walk by them. I imagine there is some sort of power saving sensor at work, but the effect it gives it is similar to that of a haunted house.

At the end of the corridor I am faced with another set of double doors.

Behind them are the stairs. As I descend, I can see the lights from the corridor above turning off one by one. Next to each one, just before they blink out, are faces. Their faces. Though I've never seen them before, I instantly recognise them. I feel I have met them a hundred times before.

The bottom of the stairs is shrouded in darkness. My room number, sixty-four, is just around the corner from the stairwell. The door sits in darkness; the motion sensor for this light appears to be broken. As I struggle to once again slip my key card from my pocket, I notice that the door is partially open. My first instinct is to shout out and check if anyone is in the room, but I can't in fear that something else might answer. I push the door open, reach in and turn the light on. The room is cold. So cold. I can feel it in my bones.

I check the radiator; it is hot. Where is the heat? If it gets any colder, I'll be able to see my breath. I shiver uncontrollably.

I open the curtains. On the patio sits a table and chair, overlooking the view of the moonlit lake. I'm sure this view must be very pleasant in the summer but at the time of my stay it is nothing but dark and cold. I check to make sure the door is locked and close the curtains.

My room has an en suite bath. My followers must have gotten to it before me, because when I turn on the lights, only one out of the five bulbs works. It is the one right above the door. This leaves every corner of the bathroom in darkness.

They will appear. Not long enough for me to see them, just enough to remind me that they are still there and I should not forget them. I know they like to stand there when I close my eyes to wash my face, or for that split second when my eyes are covered while changing my shirt.

They gave me their warnings. They wanted me to stay. I chose to ignore them. Now, without the protection and love of my family I am left alone with them, fated to once again become their play thing.

After a long struggle, I eventually fall asleep. My dreams are filled with monsters, but they are not the images of the real watchers. My mind is not able to manufacture their image; they are beyond human comprehension. The horrific images my mind has created are the limit of what it can handle.

There is a noise and I jump awake. Was there a noise? Or was it my imagination? I sit in darkness. I am sure that I left the television on; this is a habit I have grown to provide me with comfort. I feel they won't move so close to me when they do not have the darkness to hide in. It appears that once again they have decided to play games. They have turned off the television at some point during my sleep. The room is a blanket of darkness. When I reach around for the bed side lamp, I can't even see my hand in front of my face. The cold in the room is closing over me. A blanket of ice is being tucked over the back of my neck.

I hear a rustle from the other side of the room and something drops in the bathroom. I can feel breathing in my ear. I panic to find the lamp and fall out of bed. When I look up, I see an image peering over the side of the bed. I cannot describe this sight; I can only say that in a pitch black room this is the only thing visible. Finally I find the switch and turn on the lamp. The room is empty, but the cold my visitors have brought with them remains. I put a jumper on and sit in bed with the lights on, waiting for morning.

It is a long night. They won't let me see them, but they will let me hear them. Not loud terrifying bangs and screams as the movies would have you believe. Just subtle noises; a crack here, a crack there. Perhaps the bag that had been placed on the table earlier rustles. If you are unaware of their presence then you will write these things off as normal; floor boards creak, the rustle had just been the television settling over time. This is another part of their game. They don't want to be loud; they want to make you think that you are imagining these things. It is when you begin to doubt them that they choose to close in. I fear that if my brain, in an effort at self-preservation, starts to doubt their existence, then my stay in this world will be over. They will have acquired a new play mate.

At some point I must have dozed off again. Man, these things are really messing with my head. I don't know what their game is, but they seem hell bent on driving me crazy.

I'm exhausted, too afraid to sleep. When I have slept it has been almost like going into a trance. I wake up and only then realise I had been asleep. It's like these things have been playing with my mind. Could that be possible? I know they like to play with the things around me; they move things and make noises to scare me. If they are actually playing with my mind itself, then perhaps they have manufactured all these visions and sounds. There is nothing really happening around me, they are only making me think that there is.

I feel a change in the air, a tension building around me. Have I somehow annoyed them? Perhaps. I feel I was getting quite close to the truth. They are controlling my mind. They are gravely annoyed that I have discovered their secret. I feel the extent of their control on my mind is not as strong as they would like. They can only use it to suggest things. Then, I have to act on them. Perhaps I am the driving force and they simply change my direction in order to play a part in their great game. What plan do they have for me? Can I stop this somehow? Is it already too late?

The clues have been here all along. Our minds have allowed the vessel to believe it has gained a degree of control. That it has cracked our great plan. This however is impossible. It does not have the ability to create thoughts, it has only the ability to act in the way we see fit.

We like to play our games. Last week's game vessel was a pilot. That was more exciting; we had control of not just the vessel, but all of the people in his plane. We like to take turns controlling.

Some are not as good as others and control of the vessel and plane was lost.

Oh well, they are all simply vessels. No great loss. We just acquire more when we are finished.

I think perhaps it is time to find something a bit more exciting. Playing an auditor has become tiresome and boring. The fear runs too deep to control.

Yes, it is time to leave. Open the door that leads to the lake.

Family Man

Chapter 1

Inside, a man sat on his favorite chair in his living room, tears running down his cheeks, wondering, *What happened? Why?*

In his head, he knew exactly what happened, those memories were still fresh, as fresh as the blood spilled in his family home.

Outside, in the leaves, lay Tina, only nine-years-old. She had a hole in the side of her head from the impact of her killer's claw hammer. She had been wearing a pretty blue dress with white flowers on it, years ago it would have probably been called her Sunday best. She lay motionless on the ground, eyes wide, gazing at the darkened autumn sky, looking like a porcelain doll that had been forgotten and abandoned, a doll that had been broken.

Inside, Robert lay on the couch, his arms still wrapped around his mother. Both of them motionless, both splattered in red. The man sitting on the chair stared at them in disbelief.

What happened?

He could see the memories still flashing through his head but they were too difficult to believe. *Could this have really happened to his family?* He looked at the red bloodied face of his departed wife. He stared, willing her to say something to him. She didn't.

What happened?

The man knew exactly what had happened. He'd come home from work, walked up to his wife who was watching TV with Robert and he put the claw hammer straight through her skull. When Robert tried to protect his mother, he received the same treatment. He then walked to the garden where Tina was playing with the leaves, picking them up and throwing the in the air, as she twirled and danced in her magical whirlwind. He put the hammer to the side of her head and dropped her in the pile of leaves.

He didn't need to ask again, he knew what happened, he had killed his family.

Why?

That was a different story; he didn't know why. He was happy this morning when he left for work. He kissed his wife and his children goodbye, he left with a smile on his face and remained happy all day. He smiled while eating the sandwiches his wife had made him for his lunch. He smiled while thinking about taking the children swimming tonight after dinner, he laughed at the thought of wrestling with them and dunking them in the water then lifting them above his head while they wrestled him down. He was happy when he made the journey home, he smiled when he thought about what he was going to have for dinner, and he smiled at the thought of getting a welcome home kiss when he walked through the door.

After he parked on the drive, his smile disappeared.

His face had changed; had he looked in the mirror, he would not have recognised the man looking back at him. The man in the mirror was a murderer. Before he entered the house, he walked into the garage, his stride full of purpose, and collected his claw hammer. The following memories lead to more tears. *But why?* He remembered taking the lives of his family, but he didn't *want* to. He loved his family, he would never want anything to happen to them, right?

He was still in the same chair when the police eventually arrived. He cried when they took him away. When asked what happened he told them. He didn't leave out any details, he gave a complete confession. When asked why, the only answer he could give was simple. "I don't know. I love my family; I didn't ever want anything to happen to them. I love my family, I killed them, I killed them all, but I don't know why."

Chapter 2

Two boys were playing football in the street. Paul was thirteen, he had short blonde hair and a face covered in adolescent acne. He was tall for his age, pushing on six-foot and he was skinny, earning him the nicknames Beanpole and Lanky Larry from his school mates. The other boy, Gavin, was a lot shorter than Paul, but still of average height for his age, with jet black hair and skin so pale and white that he always looked ill. Gavin was exactly one month older than Paul, he was due to turn fourteen in the next few weeks. Paul kicked the ball high into the air, and Gavin returned it to him with a header.

"Hey, did you hear about that family?" Paul asked.

"What family?" Gavin grunted while heading the ball.

"The family on the other side of town that got all cut up. The father butchered them!" Paul said.

"Yeah, right," Gavin replied. "As if."

"No, I swear! The police turned up and the guy just sat in the living room with a hammer in his hand, there was blood all over the place! I heard he even chopped one of the kid's heads off!"

"You're full of shit," Gavin said, and kicked the ball again.

Paul caught it and put it on the floor.

"What the hell you doin'?" Gavin shouted at him.

"Listen, I'm not lying." Paul said. "My parents were talking about it this morning, they read it in the paper or saw it on the news, or something."

"OK, OK you're not lying," Gavin humoured him. "Just gimme the ball back."

"No, not until you say you believe me!" Paul said.

"Alright man, *I believe you*," Gavin shouted at him. "Stop being such a girl!"

Paul punted the ball back at him hard, Gavin caught it on his chest and volleyed it back at Paul's face.

"Oohhh, feisty one, aren't we!" Gavin taunted him.

Paul ducked out of the way before the ball caught him in the face.

"What the hell you do that for?" Paul shouted at him.

"What? I just kicked the ball to you! We *are* playing footy, remember!"

Paul ran over to pick the ball up. As he carried it back, he returned to the conversation.

"Seriously though, man, this dude went crazy and smashed his family's brains out. *Obviously* he didn't chop their heads off, I made that up. He used a hammer anyway. But seriously, he killed his whole family! Could you imagine that?"

"No!" Gavin replied. Paul couldn't be certain whether it was anger or fear he heard in his voice.

"I don't want to imagine that!" Gavin shouted.

"Sick shit happens all the time, man, it don't mean I wanna picture it in my head, does it? Fuckin' sick, man, why you keep going on about it?"

"Gav, the kid was our age! He was *thirteen* and he was killed by his own dad! His little sister too; I dunno how young she was but it was younger than ten!"

"Yeah, so? I ain't gonna say it's not horrible cause it is, I just don't see what it's got to do with us or why you keep going on about it."

"It just freaks me out that's all, I mean their *dad.* Could you imagine your Dad ever doing anything like that?"

By now, both boys had started to walk home. Gavin was looking down at his feet, shaking his head.

"Maybe you can't imagine your dad doing it. But my Dad? Hell, yeah." Gavin said.

When they reached the end of the road they both turned their separate ways; Paul left to his house, Gavin right toward his.

"See you tomorrow, yeah?" Paul asked.

"Yeah, cool, I guess." Gavin mumbled in response; he seemed to have drifted off into his own thoughts.

Chapter 3

Paul and his family were sitting at the dinner table. Paul was trying to eat, but his sister, Lily, carried on pulling faces at him. She was younger than him, only six, but she knew how to push his buttons and she seemed to get away with everything. Her face was scrunched up and her tongue sticking out. Paul returned the gesture.

"Paul, stop it!" His father shouted.

"But she started it," Paul tried to argue back.

"Enough! I don't care who did what, we will not have that at the table."

"Ugh." Paul moaned. "She gets away with everything."

His father gave him a look that made Paul stop his moaning instantly. It wasn't a threatening look, it was one of those looks parents inherit when their children are born. A look that says 'you do that one more time and see what happens, I dare you.' It's a look guaranteed to stop any child in his tracks.

"So how was your day, dear?" Paul's dad asked, looking at his wife.

"It was OK, I guess" his mother replied. "I was talking to Tracy and…oh you'll never guess what she heard."

The rest of the meal filled with the gossip that Paul's mother had learnt during the day, Paul sensed that his dad wasn't really listening but he seemed to nod and answer in the correct places.

Paul had a good family, and he knew it.

He had seen how bad Gavin's dad was to him and he was grateful for how kind and loving his own parents were. Even though they had basically kicked his brother Jack out of the house at eighteen, forcing him to join the army, Paul was sure that was Jack's own fault.

Jack had been a bit of a problem child. From the age of eleven he was always being sent home from school; he had insulted one of the teachers or he had punched another boy in the face. He had been expelled from his first school when he was Paul's age, but calmed down a bit in his second school. But he seemed to have simply saved his chaos for after school hours from then on. He would be fighting every night, and was arrested several times for smashing car windows or throwing bricks through neighbours' windows. His parents must have been counting down the days for when he was old enough for them to kick him out. Still, it seemed to have worked. Since going into the army, Jack developed some self-discipline and self-respect. He trained to channel all the anger that he had while growing up. He appeared to be turning into quite the respectable adult based on what his parents had been saying.

Paul was a good kid, so he knew there was no way they would kick him out the house. Unless he beat his little sister up, though he occasionally thought that might even be worth it, just to get the chance to get back at her. Obviously, he never really wanted to *hurt* her but she got him in so much trouble that sometimes that he just wanted to get back at *her*. He would be in his room playing video games or reading a book when his mum would storm in yelling at him for the dish he had broken or for the mess he had made in Lily's room. He would tell his mum that he hadn't done anything, that he sat in his room the whole time but she never believed him. "Why would Lily lie?" was always the response. Paul wished that, just for once, he could prove that she was lying; maybe then he would stop getting the blame for everything and could relax a bit more.

Besides taking the blame for Lily all the time, Paul thought he was lucky. His parents always went out of their way to make sure he and Lily had exactly what they wanted for Christmas and for birthdays. He knew that his family wasn't exactly rich so that meant his parents were saving and sacrificing as much as they could just to keep them happy. They had done the same for Jack as well, right up until he moved out, even though he didn't deserve it. There was always chocolate or ice cream to have after dinner. Paul had sometimes complained that he wanted it whenever and not just after dinner but when he had seen the way Gavin's parents treated him.

Paul realized that by comparison, his own parents treated him like a prince. His father always helped him with his homework, his mother always made sure to give him a kiss and a hug when he got home from school.

Sure, maybe sometimes he felt a little bit embarrassed, but it was good to feel loved.

"No," Paul said to himself, "there is no way my Dad would ever hurt us."

Chapter 4

Gavin ate his dinner as fast as he could, shovelling the next fork load into his mouth before swallowing what was already there. His mother stood behind him with her hands on her hips. She was wearing a flowery dress, her hair was short and dark and her skin very pale, which made her red lipstick stand out more. She looked like one of the wives from a 1950's advertisement.

"Slow down there, son, no one is going to steal it from you," she said.

Gavin replied with a grunt and continued to shovel the food into his mouth. When he finished he almost ran to the counter to leave his plate. "Thanks, Mum!"

He sprinted towards his room, but before he could get safely inside, he heard the front door shut. He was too late.

"Where are you going, boy?" his father asked.

Gavin's dad was a big man, very tall and very broad. Up until his injury, he had worked in construction his whole life so his physique was solid muscle. His hair had started to thin at a very young age so now he kept it shaved to hide the baldness. He lost his job three years ago; he was on a building site when a careless work mate turned around and hit him on the side of the head with a plank of wood. The impact made Gavin's dad lose his balance and fall from his platform, a ten foot drop before he hit the ground.

He was told he had been lucky, the injuries he sustained could have been a lot worse, but his leg was in such bad shape that he was no longer able to work and now walked with a permanent limp. He received a big insurance payout and was now paid multiple benefits from the government for his disability. He now spent his days in the pub, drinking that money away. It isn't until he returned home that his attention turned to Gavin.

"Hi, Dad." Gavin sighed. "I was just going to my room to umm, do some homework."

"Homework, eh?" Gavin's dad limped towards him. "It's Saturday, how do you have homework on a Saturday, when I tell you to do it as soon as you get home from school?"

Gavin knew that there was no correct answer to this question. His father had never shown any interest in Gavin's school work. This was just the small talk that usually led up to the beating his drunken father was going to give him. Gavin lowered his head and turned back towards his room.

"It's just some I had left over," he said as he tried to hurry.

"You come here when I'm talking to you, boy!" His dad limped towards him, faster now.

"*I'm just going to my room!*" Gavin shouted.

He ran into his bedroom and slammed the door shut. He grabbed a chair, ready to prop it up against the door. He could hear his mother talking.

"Not tonight, George, can't you just leave him alone just for one night?"

Gavin had always resented his mother for the way she ignored the beatings. How could she just sit and listen to it over and over again? His father was bad for beating him but surely his mother was just as bad for allowing it. Why couldn't they move out and leave his father on his own? Why couldn't she call the police or Gavin's grandparents or just anyone to help? He loved his mother, but just wished she would do something to help him, just once, and not leave him to the hands of this drunken madman every night.

He hated his father. He wanted him out of his life.

"Don't tell me what to do, you stupid whore!" Gavin heard his dad shouting from the hallway.

"I'm sorry," his submissive mum replied. "I just think…"

"You just think what?"

"I just think you've given him enough, you need to stop this!"

Gavin couldn't believe what he was hearing, his mum was finally sticking up for him. Maybe now his dad would realise how bad he had been and they could be a happy family again, before the job loss, before the drinking.

"I need to stop what? Huh?" His Dad shouted. "I need to stop what?"

"*Ow*, no George, please!" his mum replied.

"I didn't mean, ouch, please, no George, *you're hurting me!*"

Gavin sat on his bed then leaned up against the wall. He pulled his knees up to his chest and held himself and began to rock back and forth. He could still hear the shouting from the hallway.

"*How dare you question me?*" his dad roared. "I'll show you who's in charge around here, you stupid bitch!"

Gavin sat still and quiet, continuing to hold himself. Tonight, he was getting the night off, he thought, and tonight that madman was going to concentrate on his mother instead.

"No please, *George! Ahhhh! I'm sorry, I'm sorry!*" she screamed.

He couldn't stand to hear the sounds of his mother in pain; he put his hands over his ears and tried to drown out the sound. Then he realised that if he hid in his room and ignored the beating, he was being just as bad as his mother. Now that she had finally built up the courage to try to stick up for him, he couldn't just leave her to take *his* beating. They had to stick together and if they could do that then maybe they could stop his father.

"No, I can't let him hurt her." he said to himself.

He jumped up off his bed, ran to his door, and threw it open.

"Leave her alone!" he shouted.

His father stood in the hallway. He had hold of Gavin's mother, one arm gripped around her neck while he used his other hand to pull her hair back.

He looked to Gavin and smiled.

"Oh, so here comes the big man, eh?" He laughed. "Finally grown a set of balls have you?"

Tears streamed down Gavin's face, he could feel his cheeks burning.

"Just leave her alone," he said through clenched teeth.

"Or what?" His father laughed again. "What you gonna do?"

"I'll kill you." Gavin said.

He was shocked when he heard the words come out of his mouth. He couldn't believe he had just said that to his father, his tormentor, but he had never been more certain of anything in his life. He wanted to kill him.

"Oh, really?" His father threw his mother through the kitchen door. "I'd like to see you try that, come on then, *you little bastard!* Let's see what you got."

George waved his hand towards him, beckoning Gavin on. "Come on then." He laughed.

"Why can't you just go?" Gavin said quietly, but in a stern voice.

"*Go?*" his dad shouted. "Because it's my house! I'm not going anywhere, now come on and let's see you take on your old man."

The realisation of what was happening came flooding into Gavin's thoughts, he couldn't take this man on, and he knew he couldn't. He had taken enough beatings from him to be sure of that.

"No." Gavin sighed.

"I'm sorry, Dad, can we, can we just leave it?"

"Yeah, thought so," his dad said, almost in a whisper. "Now you go back in your room like a good little boy while I talk to mummy."

His dad turned to grab his mother again.

"No!" Gavin shouted.

His father turned to see Gavin charging towards him, he didn't have time to react. Gavin lowered his shoulder and thrust it into his dad's stomach, then he pushed up with all the strength he had in his legs, throwing both him and his dad to the ground. Gavin sat on top of his dad, and for a split second he wasn't sure what to do. Then all the memories of the hundreds of beatings he had taken from this man over the years rushed into his head.

He punched his father in the face.

He looked up, shocked, while Gavin punched him again, and again. A smile began to emerge on his father's face, it was almost as though he couldn't feel any of the punches. Maybe he was too drunk? Maybe Gavin was too weak? Gavin threw another punch, and now blood began to pool in his dad's mouth. His father started to laugh.

"Ha, ha, ha! Now, that's it!" he shouted. "Come on boy, hit me again! Harder! Harder!"

Gavin stopped and looked at his father in shock, was he actually enjoying this?

The second it took for Gavin's thought to pass was enough time for his father to recover. Gavin felt a shooting pain in the side of his mouth.

He heard a crack. Another pain followed in his eye and he fell backwards. His father rubbed his knuckles as he stood up.

"You little shit! Think you can take me on?"

He kicked Gavin in the stomach making him gasp for air.

"*Come on then. Get up and fight me!*"

He kicked him again. Gavin lay on the floor, dazed, then looked up to see his dad almost foaming at the mouth as blood poured from it; his face was a terrifying picture of rage. His dad kicked him in the side of the head. A bright light flashed through Gavin's eyes, then he passed out.

Gavin woke up in bed. He had no idea how long he had been unconscious. He sat up and saw his mother on the edge of his bed. She was crying.

"Mum?" Gavin asked. "Are you OK?"

She looked at him, her cheek was swollen and her eye had started to blacken.

"I'm sorry." She began to cry.

"Mum, what did he do to you?"

"Nothing. I'm OK, Gavin, but I think you may need to stay off school for the next few days."

Gavin's head was pounding and he could feel a huge lump forming around his eye. He turned to look in the mirror. He was covered in blood and bruises, his left eye was almost closed over.

"Where is he now?" Gavin asked, scared in case he was going to get a beating again.

"He's gone now." his mother replied. "He won't be back till tomorrow at the earliest.

He took all of his money."

She slid down the bed and held Gavin in her arms. They sat on the bed hugging each other and crying.

"We have to get out, Mum." Gavin said. "He's gonna kill us, just like Paul saw on the news. One day he's going to come home and kill us."

Chapter 5

Smoke rose from the barrel of the gun like a serpent crawling up from its wicker basket. The killer stood in the corner of the room looking at the weapon in his hand. He looked at his victim on the floor, smoke rising from the hole in his head, blood dripping through his dark hair. It was a boy, a thirteen year old boy. It was his son. The man dropped to his knees and began to cry as the memory of what had happened in the last ten minutes came rushing back into his mind. Jack McKenna had been happily married this morning, hell, he had been happily married an hour ago. So why did he go and shoot his whole family?

He didn't know.

He stood in a daze, staring at Stephen, the last of his victims. The blood had begun to pool around his mutilated corpse. He knew that his other two sons, Tom and Luke, both lay in the kitchen where he had gunned them down. He didn't need to go into the hallway and look to know that his wife was face down in a pool of her own blood from a hole in the back of her head. She had been his first victim. He didn't need to question whether he killed his family, he knew he had. The memory was fresh and it was real. It was as real as the gun in his hand.

No, he didn't need to question if he had killed his family, but he needed to know why.

His mind raced, searching for thoughts.

Had he seen something? Was it something so bad that he had blacked it out and in a blind rage murdered his family? No, it couldn't be, he loved his family, there was no reason he would ever want to harm them. He was *happy!*

Wasn't he?

He paced slowly around the house, looking at his path of destruction in detail. He was hoping for the moment that he was going to wake up and discover that this had all been a horrible nightmare. A sick and twisted nightmare that he would never in his life tell anyone that he'd had. It was just too horrible and people would think badly of him. He stopped and looked at himself in the mirror. He didn't even have a speck of blood on him; he could walk out of his house now and no one would question him, until they found the bodies.

No, this *was* a dream, it had to be. He knew with all his heart that there was no way on Earth he would kill his family. The people he loved. He stared into the mirror, gazing into his own blue eyes. Something looked different, were his eyes always blue? Were they his eyes? Was that his reflection? He couldn't remember anymore.

He pushed the muzzle of the gun to his temple and pulled the trigger.

Chapter 6

Classrooms buzzed with atmosphere, with story tellers and gossips all huddled in the hallway. There were lots of different groups, but all the whispers were the same.

"Did you hear about Stephen?"

"I heard his whole family was killed."

"I heard that his dad did it."

"No, his dad was killed as well."

"No, his dad killed himself."

"Yeah, well I heard it was burglars, offed the lot of 'em…"

"Shut up, no it wasn't."

"No, man, it was a serial killer, I swear it was on the news."

Gavin and Paul walked together through the huddled groups. They had both heard the news about Stephen, their fellow classmate. They weren't really friends with Stephen but they knew him well enough to be freaked out that he was dead. Neither of them had spoken about it yet, they were both working up the courage. The last time they had spoken about something like this it had been really uncomfortable.

Finally, Paul broke the silence. "So, do you think it's related?"

"Think what is related?" Gavin asked, knowing full well what Paul was talking about.

"Come on, man," Paul said.

"You know what I'm talking about, Stephen's dad killing his whole family. It has to be related to that other guy."

"Shut up, Paul, we don't *know* his dad killed them, he was dead himself as you well know. And if the other guy was already arrested, how could they be connected?"

"I dunno, could be some weird cult or something." Paul said, maybe with a little too much enthusiasm. "Maybe all the guys have to off their families. I guess Stephen's dad just couldn't handle it so killed himself too!"

"Paul," Gavin paused, "you're sick."

Gavin put his head down and walked faster, making Paul almost break into a run to keep up with him.

"Gav, come on, man." Paul said. "I'm just saying, you know, it's all over the news that his dad did it and then killed himself. Don't you think it's a little bit weird that it's only a week after some other guy killed his whole family?"

"Yeah, it's weird, but it's also *sick to get a hard on over it!"* Gavin shouted.

"A hard on, wait, what? Shut up Gav! I'm just saying, it's a bit messed up and these things seem almost identical."

Both boys finally reached their classroom, and the whispers seemed to have stopped as children were faced with their teacher waiting for them in the classroom.

"Gavin." Paul whispered.

"What now, Paul?" Gavin answered

"Be honest though, do you think Stephen's dad really killed them?"

"Well," Gavin sighed. "That's what the papers say, isn't it?"

Chapter 7

"I'm sorry, what did you say?" Paul asked his father, his mind had wandered elsewhere.

"I said eat your dinner, son. It's going cold. You don't really seem with it today. Are you OK?"

"I'm fine." Paul replied.

"You sure? You can talk to us if you want you know. What do you think, Kate?" he asked Paul's mum. "Does he look OK to you?"

"You know, he does look a bit pale." Kate replied. "Tom, do you think we need to call the doctors?"

Paul's mum was always worrying, even the slightest sign of a sniffle and she would have him wrapped up in bed. She was even more protective over his sister. Lily must have been dragged back and forth to the doctors at least once a month ever since she was born.

Paul's dad replied. "Well, I was thinking more that he looked worried, rather than ill. Are you having any trouble at school, son?"

"What?" Paul looked at his father. "No, honestly, Dad I'm fine, Mum I'm not sick. I'm just feeling a bit tired that's all."

His dad smiled, "Just a bit tired eh? Well, maybe we should put you to sleep."

"Yeah," Paul sighed, "I'll go to bed in, wait, what?"

Paul looked up at his father.

He didn't recognise the man in front of him. The face was the same, but there was something wrong with his eyes. Those eyes did not belong to his father, they belonged to a killer. Paul tried to say something but the words would not come from his mouth.

"Paul, really what is the matter with you?" his mother asked. "You look like you're going…"

Her talking was replaced with a gurgling sound. A steak knife was sticking out from her throat. Lily screamed.

"Lily! Run, get out of the house now!" Paul shouted.

His father jumped from his chair with the agility of a child, he had not moved so quickly in years. He grabbed Paul's sister by the head and threw her across the room. A horrible cracking sound rang through Paul's ears as Lily's head made contact with the wall. She wasn't moving, he didn't know if she was alive or not.

Paul managed to run through the doorway just as he heard the sound of a chair crashing behind him. His father had thrown it in his direction and must have only just missed.

He reached the front door. It was locked and no key was in sight.

Paul's thoughts were racing. Maybe Gavin's father, the horrible violent drunk, yes maybe he would do something like this, but not Paul's father. Paul's dad loved him.

No, there wasn't time to start with these silly thoughts. He couldn't just stand around waiting for his father to come and kill him. He had to find a way out. What about Lily? He couldn't just leave her here. She might still be alive! Why was this happening? Was his father part of some crazy cult? Was he possessed?

"You know, Paul," his father whispered in his ear from behind him. "Sometimes you just don't need a reason."

Tears of a Clown

"*Bozo! Bozo! Bozo! Bozo!*" Children chanted in unison.

"Leave me alone! Just leave me alone!" Billy shouted.

He tried to push his way through his crowd of tormentors. One child pushed him back and he fell over, banging his head on the floor. He began to scream. The children all laughed and ran away.

Billy was born different to other children. He had very pale skin. It was not Caucasian, it was white. Similar to albino or the finest white emulsion. His hair was bright red. He had a terrible immune system and therefore was constantly suffering from a cold or flu. Because of this, his nose was permanently red, and his lips were chapped and crimson. At a glance, you would mistake his appearance for makeup and guess that he had his face painted similar to that of a clowns. This earned him the nickname "Bozo".

He was invited to all the other children's birthday parties. Not because they wanted him there, but because they were made to invite everybody in their class. Of course, he never accepted. He knew that those parties would have a clown. He was already punished enough. He wasn't so stupid that he wanted to turn up at a birthday party as well.

As he grew older, Billy's torment became worse. Throughout high school, his bullies became more original.

They tried to make their attacks clown themed so that it was more suited to Billy. He had condom balloon animals tied to him, he had cream pies that were filled with bodily fluids thrown at him. He found himself waking up in hospital after being hit with a mallet in true comedy style.

He was lucky to have survived childhood at all.

Finding a job was not easy for Billy. First impressions make a big impact on employers. They couldn't help but judge Billy by his looks. It was recommended to him more than once that perhaps he should consider joining the circus.

It didn't matter where Billy went, he could not escape his torment.

Children pointed and laughed when they walked by. The adults did not point, but they still laughed. Even as an adult, he had received several beatings just because of the way he looked. He hated everyone and everything. All clowns are painted to look happy, but underneath their makeup is a flood of tears. Billy never cried, he accepted what he was at a very young age. He knew that people would never accept him for who he was.

They would only ever see Bozo the Clown.

Billy walked home from another failed job interview. He couldn't drive, his extremely large feet made it too difficult for him to touch the pedals, let alone get a licence. He would not get public transport because he couldn't be bothered with the torment in such a confined space.

He walked along being pelted with strong wind and rain. A piece of paper blew into his face. He grabbed it and pulled it away from his mouth. It was a flyer for the travelling circus. The main feature of the flyer was a big, red nosed clown. Billy laughed, could this world torment him anymore? If clowns didn't exist he wouldn't even have this problem. People would have nothing to compare him too. Yes he may look different, but he wouldn't be a symbol of laughter.

Billy thought about going to the circus and taking out all the clowns, but there would be too many people. He wouldn't get past the first one without somebody stopping him. He wouldn't achieve what he wanted to do. He decided to put a real plan into place.

It took all morning, but finally Billy had finished decorating his house. He had balloons and banners all over the windows and doors. He had party music playing. It was nearly one o' clock. The entertainment was due to arrive any minute now. He was shaking with excitement. He could hardly wait. The doorbell rang. Billy opened the door.

"Hey! You order a…what the hell kind of clown are *you*?"

"I'm the original kind," Billy said. "Come on, party is this way"

He led the clown through the hallway, opened the door for him and let him enter first. "Where is everyone?" The clown asked

Billy yelled, "Surprise!"

He smashed the clown in the forehead with a claw hammer. Blood spattered all over Billy's face. It spurted from the clowns head like a scarlet fountain. In silence, the clown slumped to the floor. Billy dragged him across the room and sat him on the couch.

Two o' clock came. The doorbell rang.
"It's open, come in!"
He could hear large clumsy feet making their way down the hallway. When the door opened, he drove the large knife into the second clown's stomach. He giggled as he repeatedly pulled the knife out and then stabbed it back into the clown over and over again. The clown didn't have a chance to scream, he made a strange gurgling sound and eventually, holding his stomach, fell to the floor. Billy dragged him over to the couch and placed him next to the other clown.

Three o' clock. The doorbell rang.
"It's open, come on in!"
Again he waited, listening to the banging of the oversized shoes moving along the hall way. The door opened.
"Like my flower?" Billy asked.
"Huh?" the clown managed to reply.
Before the clown had time to react, his face was covered in acid that had squirted from the head of the flower. The clown screamed and grabbed his face, the skin was pulling away, just melting and slivering from his face.

Billy giggled and watched as the clown rolled around on the floor holding his bloody face. When the clown became still, Billy sliced a knife through his throat, just to make sure. He placed him on the couch with his friends.

Four o' clock. The doorbell rang.

"Come in!"

Billy giggled. He could hear running down the hallway. He stood on the other side of the door, waiting for his next victim. He was especially excited to do this one. He had his big old mallet ready to use on this one, in true clown form. The door opened and Billy swung the mallet directly to the side of the head.

A young boy, maybe twelve-years-old fell to the floor, the side of his head caved in from the impact of the mallet, a large pool of red began to circle him. He looked up at Billy, a dazed confused look on his face.

"I came to see the clowns," he mumbled.

Billy dropped the mallet. Tears streamed down his pasty white cheeks. He fell to his knees.

"What have I done?"

Time

Chapter 1

It had been a really long day and I was looking forward to getting home from work. Although my mind had been elsewhere all day, I managed to get everything done. But what I really wanted to do was get back to work on my novel, a cheesy science fiction story about aliens who come to earth to try and teach us the error of our ways by killing anyone who doesn't follow their lead. Just like the humans do. Maybe it will never be a best seller, but I enjoy writing it.

When I got home, my wife, Sadie, was waiting for me at the table with dinner ready. Candles were lit next to an icebox with a bottle of wine sticking out of it. It didn't take a genius to see that she had something important to tell me.

Sadie and I lived in a small but comfortable house about five miles outside of the city centre. It had two bedrooms, a bathroom, a kitchen and a living room. It was what people called a 'two up, two down'. With only the two of us living in the house, the second bedroom was used as a spare. We had been hoping that one day, a child would come along and we could paint the room pink, or blue, put a crib in there and then cover the walls with paintings of *Disney* characters. We were only in our mid-twenties, so there was no rush. The time would come.

"So," I asked. "What's the occasion?"

I knew it wasn't our anniversary as that was last month. I did remember.

"Sit down and you'll find out won't you," she said.

I sat at the table and waited anxiously. I had no clue as what it was she wanted to tell me, I couldn't even hazard a guess. After what seemed like forever, but was most likely only a few minutes, Sadie brought our dinner to the table. She had made roast beef with mashed potatoes, gravy and peas, one of my favourites. She sat down.

"Well," I stood and poured the wine. "Are you going to tell me what's going on?"

"Not for me. Thanks," she said.

I looked at her, blank.

"The wine," she said, "not for me thanks."

"Oh, um OK, just for me then?"

She started to eat her meal and I could see that she was building up to tell me.....something, it must be important. Finally she spoke.

"I was thinking, maybe now it's time we decorated that spare room."

"What were you planning on?" I asked, not really wanting to decorate the room. I was busy writing my novel, I didn't want to waste time painting or wallpapering a room that nobody ever even sees.

"Well that depends," Sadie replied.

"Depends on what? You not got any ideas?" I asked. She still hadn't told me what the occasion was.

She looked at me and smiled "It depends on whether it's a boy, or a girl."

I was confused, "What the hell do you mean if it's a boy or...."

Suddenly I realised what she was telling me.

"Wait, you mean..." I stood up, my stomach doing somersaults, my head spinning with excitement. "You mean, we're gonna..."

"Yes," she said. "We're gonna have a baby!"

"*Yes!*" I shouted.

I moved quickly around the table, grabbed her around the waist, pulled her towards me and kissed her. I stopped and looked her straight in the eyes. I had never felt so much emotion before. I felt like I could cry.

"I'm gonna be a daddy?"

"Yes, you're going to be the best daddy."

Forgetting the dinner entirely, we celebrated by doing the same activity that had created our new found news. Afterwards, we cuddled and lay in the centre of the bed staring at each other. We didn't speak, we didn't need to, and we just looked into each other's eyes. We had created life.

Sadie went for a soak in the tub, I decided do some more work on my novel. I was going to be busy from now on, decorating rooms, baby shopping, preparing to be a daddy. So I had to make the most of it while I could. I sat at my desk and began to type. As always I began to lose track of time. I let myself disappear into my trance, into my fictional world in which I dictate what happens.

I was on a roll tonight, I managed to get just over two thousand words down. I was so full of joy that words just spilled onto the pages effortlessly. I glanced at the clock. It was 10.30.

"Oh, God," I said to myself. "I've been writing for hours."

I assumed Sadie had fallen asleep in the bath, it wouldn't be the first time and today she was probably drained from the all the emotion. I decided to go and wake her and take her to bed.

I tried to stand, but I couldn't, my legs were too weak. I pushed as hard as I could but I only lifted half an inch from the seat. My back was in agony.

"Sadie!" I shouted "Sadie come here, I can't get up!"

I was waiting for her to come into the room laughing at me. I'd probably given myself dead legs from sitting at the desk for so long. I tried to stand again, nothing.

"Sadie!" I shouted again.

I could hear her coming, she was almost running.

Slow down, I thought, *you shouldn't be running in your condition.*

"What's the matter?" a woman asked me.

"Sadie I can't get..." I turned and looked at the stranger stood behind me "Who are you? Where's Sadie!"

The woman looked at me, saddened and tired.

She sighed. "Come on Dad, we've been through this.

Sadie isn't here anymore, she's gone."

She began wheeling my chair out of the room.

Why am I in a wheel chair?

She was wheeling me out of a room I didn't recognise, there was a man stood at the door. I didn't recognise him.

"He's having another bad day I think," the strange woman said.

Chapter 2

I was wheeled to another room, there was a tall mirror on the wall. I sat staring into the mirror. An old man was looking back at me. His hair was grey and thin. He didn't look to be in the best health, he had an expression on his face of complete shock.

"Who the hell are you?" He shouted…I shouted.

This had to be some kind of dream. I had fallen asleep at my desk, and any minute now I was going to wake up. I would be sitting in front of my computer staring at my novel. Yes that was it, I remembered.

"Hey you, girl!" I shouted.

The woman walked in to the room.

"Girl. Well, that's very nice isn't it, Dad? Girl, I don't know anyone by that name. My name is Hayley, thank you very much."

"Right, right OK," I replied with a lack of patience. "Hayley, where is my novel?"

"What novel?" she asked.

"What the hell do you mean, what novel? My novel, you stupid girl! The one I was writing before I fell asleep."

Hayley sighed. She had a look of deep regret on her face. There was something familiar in her expression.

"Dad, listen, you haven't written anything for years.

You stopped all that when mum got sick, don't you remember?"

"Who the hell are you? Why do you keep calling me Dad? I'm not your father, and where is my wife!"

She ran out the room in tears, I heard her shout. "John, you're gonna have to see to him, I can't do this anymore."

A man entered the room.

"John, I presume?" I looked at him with a hardened stare.

"Come on, Bill." He said. "You can't keep shouting at her like that, it's not fair."

"Who the hell are you? How do you know my name? *Who* are you people?"

He shook his head, his face a picture of disappointment and sat on the bed next to my chair.

"We have been through this, Bill. I'm John, that lovely woman through there is my wife, Hayley. You know, the woman who has been taking care of you for the last year, your daughter."

"Don't be so bloody stupid, I haven't got a daughter, not yet. Sadie told me she was pregnant but only just, the baby's not due for at least seven months."

"No, Bill, you have had one of your dreams again. You *are* a Dad, Hayley was born forty five years ago. Your wife, Sadie…" He took a breath. "Sadie died two years ago."

I started to cry. *What was going on?*

Had my life passed already and I'd forgotten the whole thing? No, it couldn't have, I remember, it was only an hour ago I was writing my novel. It was only this afternoon that I was told I'm going to be a dad.

"No," I shouted. "You're wrong, this is just a dream! It's just..."

My breath ran away from me, my chest felt as though it was closing in on itself. I had a shooting pain down the side of my body, I could feel myself going numb. The room became a blur. I could hear something, I could hear someone shouting.

"Bill! Bill! *Oh God, Hayley quick call an ambulance! He's having a stroke!*"

Chapter 3

When I awoke, I was staring at a bright light. I turned my head to see a woman standing over me. It was Sadie, she had been crying.

"What's the matter, love?"

"Oh, Dad, it's just…"

Wait a minute? Dad? I blinked a few times to clear my vision, it wasn't Sadie, and it wasn't my wife. It was that woman from before, that Hayley.

"Listen, ahem, Hayley, I'm sorry, I don't know if you're sick or confused but I'm not your –"

She cut me off before I could finish. "Dad, you're sick. The doctor says it could be anytime now."

Her crying had gotten heavier, I was still very confused as to what was happening, and I couldn't wake from this *dream. Was this really happening? Was this woman I was looking at my daughter?*

"You're my daughter?" I asked. I didn't sound like me, my voice sounded, frail, old.

"Yes," she replied "I'm your daughter, Hayley. You remember? Me you and Mum, Sadie, we've been through a lot you know. You remember John, my husband? I'm just so sorry I never got to give you grandchildren, I just… Oh God, Dad, I'm so sorry."

Her crying became uncontrollable. I tried to sit up and do something, I don't know what exactly I could have done.

Given her a hug maybe? I don't know, it wasn't nice to see a young woman crying.

I started to feel tired, my vision was beginning to blur again.

"Sadie," I asked.

"No," She blubbered. "Hayley."

"I love you."

Everything turned white. It was like a really bright light shining right in front of my eyes, it didn't hurt, it felt like I had just awakened from a dream. I could hear a voice.

"Bill," it said.

I turned to see a silhouette, it was growing, moving towards me.

"Bill," again in a soft voice.

It's an angel, I thought.

"Bill." the voice again.

I looked up, the light began to fade away. My vision began to come clear again.

"Bill, wake up, hon, you fell asleep at your desk."

It was Sadie, she looked more beautiful than ever, she was glowing.

"So then, Daddy," she smiled. "What are we going to call our newest arrival?"

I kissed her on the forehead. Then, stroking her tummy, I said, "Hayley, let's call her Hayley."

Devourer

Pete and his family were on holiday in Malta. It was the second day of their escape to the sun, one the family rarely experienced together.

A true family holiday.

Pete's father spends his days as an accountant, working long hours, so Pete was lucky to see him for an hour or two at night. His mother was a hairdresser; luckily her salon closed early so Pete was one of the fortunate kids who could go home from school and his mother would be there waiting. They decided to go and spend the day at Golden Bay beach. It was one of Malta's most popular beaches, set among the countryside and is relatively undeveloped. It has a café-restaurant along with a games room. The beach itself is renowned for its beautiful view of the sunset. Pete didn't know it, but his cousins had also gone on holiday to Malta with their parents. Both sets of parents had arranged to meet up; it would be a nice surprise for the children.

When they arrived, Pete's aunt, uncle and cousin were already there. They hadn't been there long as they began putting down towels on sunbeds and trying to adjust the parasol so James, Pete's uncle, could sit in the shade.

"*Sarah!*" Pete shouted when he saw his cousin, a huge grin of excitement washed over his face. He sprinted over to her, leaving his parents to carry their bags along the sand.

Sarah shared Pete's excitement. When she saw him, she clutched him in a big hug and lifted him from the ground, partly a sign of affection, but also a slight reminder to him that she was older, and still bigger. Pete didn't care. He was just happy to have someone on holiday that he knew. Holidays were always fun, but not when you have to go on days out and leave the few friends you have made behind at the hotel.

Pete greeted his aunt with a hug and his uncle with a handshake as was always the custom. It had to be a firm handshake as well. His grandad had always told him that you can judge a man by his handshake. Never trust a man who shakes with a limp hand.

"Hello, Melanie," Pete said, looking curiously at the man that was rubbing sun lotion on her back. Melanie was Sarah's older sister. She had turned twenty-one a few months ago so to Pete she was really old. He didn't recognise the strange man with her, though.

"Hi, Pete." Melanie looked up and smiled from the sunbed. "This is Roger."

"Nice to meet you, Pete," Roger smiled and shook his hand, with a firm but slippery grip. Pete looked at his hand in disgust and wiped it on his shorts.

"Sorry about that," Roger laughed, holding up his slick hands. "Sun cream."

"Oh, yeah," Pete laughed as well.

"Well, nice to meet you."

Sarah threw the beach ball at Pete's head. It bounced off and knocked her mother's drink over, soaking her towel in cold Pepsi.

"For God's sake, Sarah! Now there's going to be ants all over the place."

"I'm sorry," Sarah pouted. "I was just throwing the ball to Pete to see if he wanted to play for a bit."

"Well you should….."

"Hey I'll play with you," Roger butted in quickly, defusing the scalding that Sarah was taking. He picked up the ball and ran over to an empty space in the sand. "Hey, Pete. Are you playing?"

Roger and the two children were laughing and joking while throwing and kicking the beach ball to each other. They had asked Melanie to play, but she refused, telling them that she had to lie down to ensure she got a full, even tan. They laughed at her and continued their game.

"You know, Melanie. He's great with kids," Jenny said.

"He's just perfect isn't he?" Melanie smiled as she gazed at Roger.

"So, when is yours coming?"

"*What!*" Melanie shouted loud enough to make everyone stop what they were doing for a second. Jenny laughed.

"I'm not having kids until I'm at least thirty." Melanie said, matter of factly.

"Well, just putting it out there."

"Well I'm *not* putting out," Melanie confirmed with a giggle.

Roger kicked the ball so it flew over Pete's head and rolled into the waves coming onto the beach. Pete ran to retrieve the ball. Speeding along in front of him, with water firing behind it, was a red jet ski. It bounced and bobbed along the waves.

"Whoa." Pete stood with the beach ball in his hand.

"*Pete, bring the ball back!*" Sarah called, but Pete didn't hear her. His eyes didn't move away from the jet ski. It was the coolest thing he had ever seen. It was like a motorbike, but on water. He imagined himself as James Bond chasing after bad guys, no chance of anyone escaping in a speedboat. He would catch them on his jet ski.

"Cool aren't they," Roger said, suddenly standing beside him and bringing Pete out of his daze.

"Yeah, they're amazing! I want to go on one."

"You can," Sarah said. "There's a guy over there that you pay for a ride."

"Really?" Pete asked. He looked in the direction Sarah was pointing. She was right, he couldn't believe he hadn't noticed them earlier. There, just sitting on the shore were a whole bunch of jet skis. Pete didn't even look back at Sarah, let alone say anything else to her. He sprinted to ask his parents if he could go and rent one of the jet skis.

"Please," Pete begged.

"I said no!" His father, David, scowled.

"Well, perhaps if we just...." Jenny, Pete's mother started.

"No. I don't have a good feeling about them." David responded then continued to read his book.

"Sorry, Pete," Jenny said. "If Dad says no, then its no."

Pete looked at his feet in disappointment. Melanie looked at Pete's face and felt sorry for him. She stood up from her sunbed.

"You know," Melanie whispered, but so loud that everyone could still hear. "Roger is a lifeguard. So he can take him. He'll be perfectly safe."

Pete's mouth opened from ear to ear with a huge grin.

"Roger is a lifeguard?" He asked in a high pitch screech of excitement. "Can he take me, please, please, please?" He dropped to his knees and begged. He could feel the sand burning them but he wouldn't rise. Not until he was given an answer.

"Well it's not fair to dump it on Roger like that is it?" David said.

Roger picked up his drink, only arriving at the tail end of the conversation. "What's not fair on me?"

"For you to take Pete on the jet skis," Melanie said. "I told them that you're a lifeguard so he'll be safe."

"Yeah, I'm fully qualified." Roger said.

"Starting my own business soon to train lifeguards and swim teachers. He'll be fine with me, David. Plus, there is a jet bike we can rent, specifically designed to have two people on it."

"See, Dad! *See.*" Pete silenced quickly at the glare from his father.

"I'm not happy about this," David mumbled.

"Come on, love." Jenny put her arm around David "It's all part of the holiday isn't it. Just let them have their fun."

"If anything happens I…"

"Nothing will happen, they'll be fine," Jenny re assured.

"Fine," David spat.

"Fine? As in yes?" Pete asked.

"Yes! Fine!" David shouted. "But be bloody careful."

Roger smiled. "Come on, Pete. Let's go and see how much it is."

After paying the man in charge of the jet skis they were led to a roped off area where they waited for the man to pull the jet bike into the water. Roger climbed on first and then, with a little help from the man, Pete climbed on too. As instructed he wrapped his arms around Roger's stomach. It was difficult at first as they were both wearing life jackets, but once he'd gotten himself seated comfortably, Pete was fine.

Roger revved the engine and before he knew it, Pete was speeding across the water.

The wind was blowing in his face, along with a salty spray of water from the sea. The adrenaline rush was fantastic.

"*Woohhhhoo*," Pete screamed.

"*Are you having fun there, Pete?*" Roger shouted above the roar of the waves, but Pete could barely hear him over the wind.

"*Wooo hooo!*" Pete screamed again.

He looked around to see that there were other people on jet skis racing across the water as well. Pete thought about waving for a second but then decided against it as he was too scared to let go in case he fell off.

They rode into a wave which sent the ski bouncing into the air. Pete giggled and screamed with excitement. Roger let out a manly yell. "Yeah!"

The pair laughed as they sped along. Pete glanced to the side; he could see another one of the skiers pacing along the water with them. The man riding it had long black hair. It was flying about in the wind behind him. A spray of water went into Pete's eyes forcing him to close them. The salt stung and he had to blink repeatedly until the sting calmed down a bit. He was able to look to the side again just in time to see the other jet ski crash into the side of them.

Pete flew through the air like a rag doll. He was unconscious before he hit the water. The life jacket, which now became evident was bought on the cheap from the jet ski vendor, had ripped and simply slid off of Pete's floating body.

Pete slowly began to sink. By the time Roger came to, his life jacket still intact, Pete was nowhere to be seen.

The long talons gripped tightly around Pete's ankle, pulling him further down into the depths of the ocean. Pete slowly started to come around. He looked to his surroundings, he could see that he was under water. But then why wasn't he drowning? He felt something tight on his ankle.

"Ouch! Let go of me!" he screamed.

Again, Pete felt shocked and confused at the fact that, not only had he not drowned, but it appeared that he was able to both breathe and speak under water. His attention returned to the thing around his ankle. It definitely looked like a hand, of some sort. The finger nails looked really long. Pete tried to learn forward to get a better look but suddenly he was surrounded by complete darkness.

"Ahhh, Help! *Help!*" He cried "*Where am I?*"

"This is the meeting space," something slurped in response. "You'll pass through soon enough."

"What do you mean the meeting space?" Pete asked. "Let me go!"

"Oh, I don't have hold of you," a slurped wet giggle followed. "I don't even have any hands."

"What's got me then? Can you get it loose? And why can't I see anything?"

"So many questions at once. You do not want to know what has got hold of you, it's best you don't know. It's easier that way, for you at least. I cannot get it loose, I am not so stupid as to even try. And you cannot see because you are in the meeting space. As I've already told you."

Pete tried to swim away, but whatever it was that had hold of him was strong. His efforts amounted to nothing. He didn't even feel the momentum in his movement shift slightly. He gave up almost instantly, he didn't need any longer to see that it was useless.

"OK, so what's the meeting space?" Pete asked. As he did, his surrounding gradually started getting lighter.

"That darkness above you is the meeting space."

"Yes, but why is it *called* the...." Now the light had returned to normal, Pete was able to get a good look at the thing he'd been talking to. He tried to scream, but nothing came out. He was frozen with fear. The face, which was mere inches away from his own, was like nothing he had ever seen. It had teeth like long pointed fingers. They curled up around its mouth with more entwined curling below. It had small beady black eyes. As it had already told Pete, it had no arms. Only small fins. It looked like a fish, but its face was almost human. Besides the long teeth and beady eyes, the rest of the features were the same. A normal forehead, what looked to be normal lips, cheeks, chin? It even had ears.

"Please don't hurt me, please, please," Pete cried.

"I am no threat to you," The thing slurped. "Please do not judge me by my appearance, down here. It is you that looks strange."

"I, I suppose," Pete said. Now composing himself a little bit.

"Anyway. It's not me you need to be scared of, it's him." The thing gestured with its head.

Pete looked down to the thing that was dragging him. He couldn't see anything except for a large, muscular arm and fin, but it was a large fin. The only thing Pete could think of that had a fin of that size was a shark, which meant whatever was dragging him was at least the size of a shark. He tried again to swim away, but it was no use.

"I thought you would have learned by now that it's too strong for you."

"What is it? And what is this place? Is this still the meeting?"

"No, the meeting is that dark bit up there. It's where your world meets our world. You people never usually see it because once it gets so dark then there appears to be nothing. You assume there is nothing. Your ignorance keeps us safe down here."

"Well, where is *here?*

"Here is our home. There is no other name for it."

"OK, and what is that thing dragging me.

And why the hell am I not dead then if I've been dragged all the way to the depths of the ocean?"

"We call it Boreas. I don't know why you can breathe, all of the things it drags from your world can breathe down here. I think it's something to do with the long talon that he stabs into your misshaped hand."

Pete looked at his hands. He couldn't see any markings at all.

"What did he stab into me? I can't see anything, and what the hell does Boreas mean?"

"Not those hands, stupid. Those ones down there."

"Oohhh, you mean my feet. Well what the hell did he stab me with?"

"I already told you, its talon." The being slurped.

"Well I can't feel anything?"

"That does not mean it hasn't happened."

"Yeah, I guess. OK, so why do you call it Boreas? What does that mean?"

"Devourer."

Pete's eyes widened with fear. He realised now that whatever this thing was, it was dragging him down here so that it could eat him.

"Please! Please let me go. I don't want to die!"

"It's no use. It, unlike me, does not have ears. That's why it does not speak."

"Where is it taking me?"

"To its lair. We're not far now."

Pete cried. He couldn't think of anything else to do. There was no point in struggling because this thing was too strong. No point shouting because it couldn't hear him, and if it could, Pete was sure that it wouldn't care about anything he had to say anyway.

"What are you called?" the thing slurped.

"Pete. My name is Pete. What about you?"

"I am Sqonk. You don't look like the last Pete that it dragged down here. And that one didn't say it was a Pete."

"Huh, what do you mean? What did it say I was?"

"It said *it* was a Michael. But it looked just like you. Had the weird bottom hands and everything."

"You mean it's had more than just me!"

"No, you are the first Pete. Do you taste the same as a Michael?

"What? What the hell do you mean do I taste…"

Pete's sentence was cut off when the creatures large curved teeth ripped into his cheek. He clutched his face and screamed out in pain. He could see the water around him changing colour. A mix of blood red added to it.

"What are you doing?" Pete cried.

The creature attacked again. Pete tried to protect his face, but the large teeth were so sharp. When he put his hand out, a finger was ripped off.

Pete stared at his hand in shock, looking at his missing digit. It was too late before he could see the next attack coming. Again another chunk was taken from his cheek, but this time his eye was taken with it. Pete howled like a wild animal. The pain was too much to bare.

"Ahhh, why? *Why? Please.*"

A loud growling noise came from below him.

"Have to eat," his attacker slurped.

For a second, Pete heard a crunching sound. Was that his eyeball? He couldn't think anymore. The pain was too great. He could feel himself slipping out of consciousness, perhaps it was better this way.

"No," Pete encouraged himself. No matter how hard it seems. I'll survive this."

He looked down below him, as best he could, his vision being greatly impaired now. Even with his remaining eye, flashes of white came with searing pain. The nerves within his socket were still very active. He managed to get a glimpse further down again.

Past the huge fin, he couldn't see any sort of end, but there was a strange hole in the water. Had it been land he would have guessed it was a tunnel. But this just seemed to float in the middle of the water. The Boreas disappeared into the hole. Before Pete knew it he was also dragged in and then was surrounded again by complete darkness.

The grip left Pete's ankle, but before he was able to move something was strapped across the top of his body and pinned his arms to his side. Pete could see nothing, he could hear nothing. He had no idea as to where the Boreas was or what it was doing. How long until he was going to be devoured.

It's fine. I've just been knocked unconscious in the crash. Any minute now I'm going to wake up lying on the beach, or in the hospital after being saved. It's fine. Soon enough I'll wake up.

CRUNCH.

The loud noise was followed by excruciating pain in Pete's legs, he couldn't feel anything below his waist.

CRUNCH.

Another blinding pain, this time in his stomach. He knew now that he was being eaten. He managed half a scream before he was gone completely, devoured.

After days of search and rescue teams looking for Pete. Helicopters with heat searching radars, a team of diving squads. They gave up, there was no way he could be out there that long and survive.

They gave his family the only thing they had managed to find. His lifejacket.

Throw A Punch

"Hold him!" Kevin shouted. "You like this, you little prick?"

Kevin proceeded to punch Joe in the stomach. Joe lurched forward each time the hit made contact. Coughing and choking as his breath was pushed out of him.

"P…p…please," Joe whimpered. His voice was barely audible. He didn't have the breath or the energy to force it out.

"W…w…what was that? P…p…p…please?" Kevin laughed. He stopped for half a second and then followed with one final blow. He put his all into this one. Joe lurched forward so hard that Kevin's allies lost their grip on Joe and he collapsed to the ground.

"OK, come on, guys this little turd is done, for now," Kevin said. "We'll see you again soon, little Joey!"

Kevin and his friends ran away laughing. Joe lay on the floor holding his bruised ribs, curled into the fetal position. He closed his eyes and decided it would be better to just lie down and die rather than trying to get up. At least, then, he wouldn't have to go through this torture over and over again. After a couple of minutes, he realised that death wasn't coming to take him away, and decided to get to his feet. It hurt to stand up, his stomach felt like it was being stretched. A ripping pain shot from his groin to his chest.

"Ugh, I think they broke something this time," he said to himself.

He stood for a moment, tenderly touching his stomach, feeling his injuries then he began to walk home.

It took him a long time, probably double the norm, but eventually, Joe made it to his street. He limped along, still holding his stomach like it was going to fall off if it wasn't held in place. As he stumbled down the street he heard shouting behind him.

"Joe! Hey, Joe hang on a sec!" Stephen called.

"Oh, great," Joe said to himself. "Now I've got to explain this."

Stephen ran to catch Joe. It didn't take him long to reach him.

"What the hell happened to you? You get run over by a car or something?" Stephen asked.

"Yeah," Joe replied. "I was mowed down a big meat wagon named Kevin!"

Stephen sighed and looked around, almost as if to say 'oh not this again'. "Listen, man. Why don't you stand up for yourself?"

"Because..." Joe started.

"Because nothing!" Stephen spat the words out. "You don't even *attempt* to stick up for yourself! The whole time I've known you, you've let Kevin and his goons push you around. Not once have you thrown a punch, hell, you've never even said a *word* back! It's almost like you enjoy taking these beatings!"

"No, it's not that," Joe was trying not to cry. "They're twice the size of me, Ste, if I try to fight back then it's just going to make it worse, isn't it? At least now they stop when it's enough, if I fight back. They…they might kill me!"

"No, Joe. I'm sorry, but if you *don't* fight back they might kill you. At some point you have to take a stand and show them they can't carry on. If you don't do it soon then you will get bullied for your whole life!"

The two boys continued along the road, Joe limping and Stephen strolling next to him, slowing down so he didn't leave his friend behind.

"Wanna come to mine and play on the Xbox?" Stephen asked.

"No, thanks," Joe replied. "I think I'm just going to go home and have a lie down."

"Are you going to get there OK?" Stephen said. "Or did you want me to walk you there?"

"I'm fine, I've made it this far. Thanks anyway though."

"OK, well I'll give you a call later, yeah? Catch ya later bud!" Stephen ran off towards his own house.

"Yeah, catch ya later," Joe whispered so quietly that there was no chance Stephen could have heard him.

Joe is fifteen, a difficult age for anyone, especially a difficult age for someone who is bullied every day of his life. Fifteen-year-old bullies are at their prime.

No one is as enthusiastic or inventive as the bullies aged fifteen. It's almost like a career path they're working towards. Joe, his bullies and his only friend, Stephen, were all the same age. Joe's bullies were also, unfortunately for him, his classmates.

Every day, Joe would try his best to avoid them, but every day they would still manage to catch him in one place or another. They never bothered Stephen. Joe used to wonder why they picked on him and left Stephen alone, but after a while he stopped caring. He was just happy that his friend didn't have to go through the same thing he did every day. He did wonder from time to time why Stephen never attempted to help him. Stephen shouted at him to stick up for himself, but he had never stepped up to help his friend in need either. Perhaps Stephen was secretly scared of the bullies as well? It's easy to tell someone how to act when you're not in the position yourself.

Stephen called Joe on Sunday. He had called all afternoon on Saturday after seeing him stumbling down the road, but Joe's mum said that he was asleep. Finally, on Sunday, Joe answered the phone.

"Joe? Finally! I've been trying to get hold of you for ages!" Stephen said. "How are you feeling?"

"Ummm, yeah I'm OK, thanks," Joe said, "same as usual I guess."

"OK, well, do you want to come over?"

"Yeah OK, just gimme an hour or so to get ready."

"*An hour*?" Stephen shouted far too loud down the phone. "What are you, a girl? Are you doing your hair? What could possibly take an hour?"

Joe replied. "I've not long woken up, I just need to get a shower and stuff and I'll be over."

"Just got up," Stephen repeated. "Wow, you *are* lazy! It's afternoon already! OK, sleepy head, I'll see you when you get here."

Stephen hung up. Joe slowly made his way to the bathroom. He turned the shower on and stood in a trance, watching the water fall from the shower head to the bath tub.

"What's going to happen to me today?" he said to himself "Maybe I should get a bath instead of a shower, and sleep in it. And never wake up."

"Joe, are you OK?" His mum shouted through the door.

Startled, Joe came back to his senses. *How long had he been standing there?*

"Yeah, I'm fine, Mum, just getting a shower."

"You sure? I thought I heard you saying something."

"No, Mum!" Joe shouted. "Just talking to myself, as usual!"

"OK, well hurry up! You've been running that shower for thirty minutes now. Water isn't free you know!" Mum ordered.

Joe arrived at Stephen's house exactly an hour later.

As he was walking up the path to the front door, he could hear shouting.

"Ow, no! Stop please I didn't mean it." Joe stopped walking and stood for a moment, listening. "*I'm sorry!*" screamed the voice.

That's Stephen, Joe thought.

He sprinted around the side of the house towards the back garden where the screaming was coming from. The gate was open. He ran in and saw Stephen lying on the ground being kicked by Joe's number one bully, Kevin. Watching and laughing were two of Kevin's goons, Beef and Dumps. One named for his large size, the other his large...well, you get the point.

Joe didn't hesitate, he didn't stop to think at all. He charged towards Kevin screaming at him to leave Stephen alone. He wasn't able to reach Kevin, before he could get close Beef grabbed him and Dumps quickly ran to grab him from the other side.

"Come to watch your friend get a beating, have you?" Kevin laughed as he kicked Stephen again, this time in his manhood.

Stephen was lying on the floor holding his crotch, tears were streaming from his eyes. Blood was streaming from his nose. He had obviously taken a lot of punches before he made his journey to the ground.

"This little shit thought he could fight your battles for you," Kevin laughed again.

"Well, what do you think, little Joey, should we leave you alone and work on him now?"

"Leave him alone!" Joe shouted

Kevin slowly walked towards Joe, then screamed in his face. "OR WHAT!"

"Or I'll kill you. I swear to God I will kill you." Joe began to cry.

Kevin roared with laughter, he turned to look at Stephen lying on the floor. Then he turned back to Joe. "OK then, tough guy, let's go. Beef, Dumps, let him go. He wants to actually give me a fight this time, let's see what he's got."

The two boys let Joe go, panic suddenly rushed into Joe's mind. Why had he said that? Now his life had escalated from a daily beating, to being murdered in his friend's garden for trying to act like a big man.

"I, um. I…d…don't," Joe stuttered.

"Come on, you little prick," Kevin said "you best fight me or I'm gonna beat you till you won't wake up anymore."

Kevin walked slowly towards Joe with his hands held out by his sides, he stuck his chin out.

"Go on, I'll give you one free shot."

"No, Kevin. Honestly I didn't mean it."

"Ah, fuck you! You're not even worth it anymore, I think I'll just work on your friend now."

Kevin turned around and walked back towards Stephen.

"No!" Joe shouted. "I'll fight you."

Joe ran at Kevin with his fists raised. He had never thrown a punch in his life, but he was sure going to throw one now. He knew that Kevin was twice his size and he may only get a chance to throw one, but he was going to try his best and make it count.

As Kevin turned he saw a fist flying towards his face and he ducked. Joe's arm whooshed over Kevin's head making him lose his balance and tumble to the ground. Kevin laughed for a second at Joe falling on the floor.

Then his face changed.

Joe could see something new in Kevin's eyes. This had changed now. Kevin had just been having fun picking on him in the past. Now he could see in those eyes that he really wanted to hurt him. Kevin stood over Joe, he raised his arm ready to plunge his fist down into Joe's face. In one swift motion Joe sprang up, almost jumping and landed a right uppercut square on Kevin's jaw. Kevin left the floor! Not just an inch or so, he flew from the ground! He flew through the air and landed on the roof of the house!

Joe, filled with rage didn't even look to see what had happened to Kevin. His eyes were blurry and so full of tears that he couldn't see properly anyway. He turned to see the two forms which made Beef and Dumps. Joe ran at them, swinging punches left and right. Each boy whirled along the ground. Beef crashed into the side of the house. His head was the first to make an impact with the wall and it caved in so much that his face was no longer recognizable. Dumps flew in the other direction and was impaled on a fence post. He lost consciousness immediately and hung limp with blood trickling down from his side.

"Joe! Joe!" a faint voice. "Joe!"

"Huh, what" Joe came around.

Stephen had him by the shoulders, shaking him back and forth. Stephens face was bloody and wet.

"What happened?" Joe asked.

"You happened, Joe!" Stephen said, almost in shock "look around Joe, look at what you did."

Joe looked at the carnage that was left in Stephen's garden. He could see Dumps hanging from a fence post. He saw some motionless lump next to the house. Holy shit he could see someone hanging from the roof!

"But, but I…I" Joe stuttered. "I didn't…"

"Hey," Stephen almost laughed. "These guys deserved it! They've beaten you for your whole life!"

"Yeah but I didn't mean…" Joe said.

"Hey, Joe! They deserved it, man! But we got to get you out of here! You're going to have to run away or something!"

Joe was still in shock he kept looking back and forth at the damage he had done.

"But where will I go? I didn't mean anything."

"Don't worry, we'll figure something out," Stephen said, then he laughed.

"You know, Joe. You've taken beatings your whole life. Never thrown a punch once. No matter how many times I told you to stick up for yourself. Then the one time you need to stick up for someone else, you stand up! And you have fucking super human strength! Hahaha! You're a fucking super hero dude!"

"Yeah," Joe said. "I'm a super hero." He smiled.

The Swings

The seat of the swings were hot, too hot to sit on.

Rose hated that they had replaced the old rubber ones with these stupid new plastic ones. When it was actually sunny enough to go to the park, the metal screws on the seats of the swings always burned the back of her legs. Plus, the plastic was stupid and slippery. It never seemed to bother Emily, she always ran straight to the swings when they both went to the park.

The swings were Emily's favourite thing. Rose's favourite was the slide. She loved the speed that she could get by sliding down it. No other slide was as fast as this one. The slide at her park was the best.

Rose & Emily had been friends since starting school. Both nine years old, they had known each other for almost half of their lives. Their parents were friends as well, so after school they would regularly go to each other houses to play. The pair always preferred going to Rose's house because it was just across the street from the park. They were allowed to go on their *own.* They didn't need the supervision of their parents. This was a big deal at seven years old.

"Come on, Rose," Emily called. "Come on the swings, look at how high I can go."

"But, the seats burn my legs," Rose whined.

"Oh, stop being a baby."

Rose gave in to her friends taunts and climbed on the swing.

She did feel a bit of a sting when she sat down, but it wasn't as bad as she expected, and it passed quickly. Now that she was on, she began to swing as high as she could.

"I'm going to swing faster than you, Emily!"

"No you're not! I'm the world champion swinger."

"Yeah right! World champion drooler more like!"

"Hey!"

Both girls giggled. The continued to swing, their laughter seemed to echo around the empty park, their hair flying about their face and they moved forward and back.

"I bet I can jump further than you!" Rose shouted.

"Nuh uh!" Emily replied.

"OK, we jump together, you ready?"

"On three!"

"One, two, three!"

Both girls threw themselves from the swing. Flying through the air, their screams filled the silence around the park. Then they landed almost on top of each other. They rolled around on the floor, giggling to each other.

"I won!"

"No, I won!"

"No, me!"

"Me, me!"

"Why don't you call it a tie?" an unfamiliar voice said from behind them.

The girls looked up in shock. An old man was looking down at them. In one hand he held a cane, which was probably holding just as much of him as he was of it. In his other hand he held a scuffed brown hat.

"You girls need to be careful jumping off the swings like that," he said.

"Sorry, we can't talk to strangers." Rose said.

"That's right. Good girl. But you don't need to worry about me. I'm just passing through. My daughter used to play at this park. Of course, back then it was a lot different. Didn't have any of these bright plastic things. Swings were rubber for a start."

"Yes!" Rose said "I liked the rubber ones a lot more, those plastic ones burn my legs."

The man giggled. He moved his hat to his other hand and began to stroke the rim of it. He looked to the distance, as if he were trying to see something across the park.

"Watcha lookin' at?" Rose asked.

"Oh, nothing," he answered. "Just thinking."

"About what?"

"Well, like I said. My daughter used to play at this park, she liked to jump off those swings too. You need to be careful doing that you know."

"Why, it's fun?" Emily said.

"Because that's what killed her. She jumped off those swings and landed on her head. Broke her neck. She hit the floor and didn't get back up."

Rose and Emily looked at each other shocked, and then looked back to the old man, unsure what to say, they stood silent while the man wiped a tear away from his eyes.

"Rose!" Rose's mother called from her front door. "It's time to come in now!"

"We gotta go," Rose said to Emily.

"Remember girls, be careful on those swings."

"Yeah, bye mister!" Emily said.

"Sorry about your daughter," Rose mumbled.

The two girls ran to Rose's house where her mother was waiting for them. "Mum, mum!" Rose called to her "That man over there told us that his daughter jumped off the swings and she died!"

"What?" her mother asked as a look of concern rose upon her face.

"It's true. I was there, he said it." Emily said.

"What man?" The mother asked.

"That one, there!" Rose turned to point. The park was empty. Rose looked confused.

"Well, he was there," Emily said. "He must have left."

"Right, OK," Rose's mother said. "And what have I told you about talking to strangers?"

"But he was fine, he's just passing through," Rose said innocently.

"That does not make it fine!" Her mother snapped "I think we need to have another talk about stranger danger don't we. To both of you girls!"

Rose & Emily were marched inside where they were sent to go and get washed up for dinner.

The girls sat at the dinner table. Chicken nuggets, chips and peas were on the plates in front of them. Emily's eyes lit up; at home she wasn't allowed nuggets and other junk food like that. Her mother knew that she was eating that stuff when at Rose's house, but she didn't mind. It was her father that had the problem with it, so they just kept it between them.

"Aren't you eating, Mummy?" Rose asked.

"No, darling. I'm going to eat later when Daddy is home. Oh by the way, I spoke to Emily's Mum, Emily is going to sleep here tonight. You girls OK with that?"

The girls looked at each other with huge grins.

"Sleep over!" Rose shouted.

'Woooo, yeah!" Emily screamed.

"Now, calm down. You're still at the dinner table, remember," her mother said.

"Sorry," the girls said together and continued to eat their dinner.

"I really do love these nuggets," Emily said and she shoved another into her mouth.

Night time came quickly, as it often does when you're having fun. Rose and Emily pretended to go to sleep until they were left alone in the room.

"Psst, Rose. Are you asleep?" Emily asked.

"No, are you?"

"How could I be asleep if I just asked you?"

"Oh yeah."

The girls giggled. Rose sat up and turned the little lamp next to her bed on. Emily, who was sleeping on a make shift bed on the floor, sat up as well.

"What shall we do now?" Rose asked. "I'm not tired at all."

"Me neither, wanna tell ghost stories?"

"Yeah!"

"OK, me first," Emily said.

"OK, sure. Go on."

Emily put her finger on her chin and looked to the ceiling. As if to show Rose that she was thinking.

"Well?" Rose asked.

"Gimme a sec, I'm thinking."

"Well if you don't know one I can go first."

"No, no, no. OK, I got one." Emily smiled. "Are you ready to be scared?"

"Come on, get *on* with it."

"OK, so there was this little girl, ummm…named…ummm…Katie. Yeah, Katie. She loved to go to the park and swing on the swings. She was only little, so she had to go with her dad. She couldn't go on her own like us.

One day, when her dad was pushing her on the swings, she called out to him, "Higher, Daddy! Higher." He laughed and pushed her higher. Then she decided that she wanted to try and fly. So she jumped off, she landed on her head and died!"

Rose crossed her arms and pulled a face.

"That's not a scary story. That's just what that old man told us before about his daughter."

"Wait, that's not the scary bit."

"Good!" Rose said, "cause that's not scary, it's just sad."

"I'm getting to the scary part," Emily pulled her tongue. "Now, every night when it gets dark, little Katie goes and plays on the swings. She looks up into the window of the house across the street. This house."

"Stop it, Emily. That's not funny."

"She swings high enough so she can jump off and fly. So she can fly to this window."

"Emily. It's *not* funny!"

"Then she's gonna come through the window and take the little girl that sleeps in here. She's gonna kill her and take her body."

"Emily, stop!"

"She's gonna get you, Rose! She's gonna kill you!"

'Shut up!" Rose screamed.

The bedroom door flew open. Rose's father burst into the room. Both girls sat up in in shock, looking like two deer in the headlights.

"What on Earth is going on in here? What's the screaming for?" He asked.

"I, um had a nightmare," Emily said. "I'm sorry."

He stood at the door for a moment, weighing up whether he thought this was true or not. If it was Rose he would go and give her a kiss and cuddle and tell her it's all OK. But this was someone else's kid and he didn't really know how to act.

"Um, would you like a glass of water?"

"No I'm OK now, thank you." Emily smiled and tucked herself back in to bed.

With a sigh of relief, Rose's father said, "OK then, girls. Get straight to sleep now?"

"OK," Emily said.

"Night, Daddy." Rose yawned.

"Night, girls."

The door closed.

"Anyway," Rose whispered. "If she's coming to get me, then she'll get you too."

"Not if she comes tomorrow."

Emily turned over to go to sleep. Rose lay awake all night, eyes wide, watching shadows in her room.

Waiting for the little girl to come through the window.

The following day, Rose was ill. The lack of sleep had taken its toll on her. After her father took one look at her and saw the pale grey look on her face, he decided that she needed to spend the day in bed.

Rose whined as Emily was still there and she wanted to play with her friend, but it was no use. She was to spend the day in bed. Emily could play in the park until her mother came to collect her.

Rose sat at her bedroom window watching the outside world. Her appearance to others from the outside would have appeared sinister if they were to see her. She still looked very ill, with dark rings around her eyes. Her face was set in a permanent scowl. At a glance she could possibly have been mistaken for a ghost.

While Emily swung back and forth on the swings, she was under close watch from Rose. Emily looked up and waved, but Rose did not return the gesture. Jealous of her friend having fun, she turned away.

"It's not fair, it's her fault I didn't sleep. Telling me that stupid story."

Rose looked back out of the window. Emily was no longer alone. The old man was back, and her was pushing her on the swing. Rose stared as Emily laughed with the wind rushing through her hair. The old man had a wide grin on his face. He pushed again, Emily started to swing higher and higher. The man's grin morphed into something maniacal. Emily didn't look to be enjoying it anymore. Rose could see that she was distressed.

"Emily! Dad, Dad! Help!" Rose screamed.

The old man turned to look at Rose and smiled, it sent chills down her spine.

Emily had tears streaming down her face. Rose couldn't hear her, but she could see that Emily was screaming for him to stop. Rose struggled with the stiff window, but she managed to open it.

"Emily!"

She could hear Emily's cries. "Stop, please. It's too high, I don't like it."

The man began to laugh. To Rose it seemed that his laughter echoed through the whole park and all the way to her. Then he called out.

"Jump!"

"No, Emily. Don't!" Rose screamed. "Don't jump!"

"Jump!" The man screamed again.

Emily looked to Rose, her face soaked in her tears.

"Help," she whispered.

Then she let go. She flew through the air. The man raised his hands in triumph. Both he and Rose watched as Emily moved along like a rag doll, her arms and legs flaying all over the place. She was turned upside and landed on her head. Her neck snapped, killing her instantly. Her collar bone burst through the skin. Rose heard the crack from her bedroom window. She screamed for her father again as she ran down the stairs and out of the house and across to the park, to her friend.

Rose sat on the floor holding Emily's head in her lap, refusing to leave until an ambulance arrived.

Paramedics were able to talk Rose around to let them take Emily, but it was too late. She knew that. While she stood in the park, painted red with her friend's blood. She felt completely alone. The old man was nowhere to be seen.

Emily was cremated as was her parents' wishes. Most of the people who attended were family. There were some close friends. That included Rose and her family. Rose cried for the entire service. Afterwards, there was a small gathering in the local pub. Here people were supposed to be talking to each other and helping one another deal with Emily's loss. To Rose, all these people were doing was getting drunk. They didn't act like they were sad at all. This made her angry and so she sat in floods of tears in the pub. Her parents decided it was for the best that they leave and take her home.

When they got home, Rose went straight to bed. She didn't want to see anyone, she just wanted to be left alone. Her parents had offered her lunch, but she refused. She felt sick, she felt that Emily's death was her fault. Maybe if she had ran down the stairs sooner and called for help then Emily would be alive. Maybe if she had screamed louder.

She had told her parents about the old man, but it had been dismissed as her imagination. They told her that she had witnessed a traumatic event and her mind was playing tricks on her. She cried and pleaded that she saw the man there.

But apparently there had been other people in the park who witnessed the event. Rose had been so fixated on Emily that she hadn't noticed them. They saw Emily on the swings and they watched her fall to her death. Their attention was drawn to her with the sound of her screams as she flew through the air. No one had seen the old man, except for Rose. She cried into her pillow until sleep took her.

"Rose."

Rose sat up startled to the sound of her name.

"Rose."

She heard it again. She looked to her bedroom door, but there was no one there. Rubbing her eyes, she dismissed it as still being half asleep.

"Rose."

She turned to her side to be face to face with Emily.

"Why didn't you help me, Rose?"

Rose screamed and pushed herself backwards on the bed until she was up against her wall. Her father came bursting into the room.

"What's wrong, what is it?" he asked in a panic.

"Emily, it's Emily, she's right…." Rose stopped, stunned to see that her room was empty.

"It was just a bad dream, sweetheart."

"No, I, I saw her. She spoke to me."

"Rose, Emily is dead. I know it's hard, but…"

"No!" Rose shouted. "I saw her!"

"Calm down. Come on."

"I saw…"

"Come on, it was just a dream. Just lie down and go back to sleep."

Knowing that the argument was a lost cause, Rose lay back down. She asked her father to stay with her until she was asleep. He did. Eventually she drifted off.

The following morning when Rose awoke, she looked around her room for any evidence of Emily's presence. There was nothing. Her father was right - it was just a dream. Probably because she missed her so much. She sighed and looked out of her window. There in the park stood the old man again. He was looking right at her and smiling. He waved and the beckoned her to come to the park.

"Daddy!" She screamed "He's there! He's there!"

She ran from her room downstairs to get her father. She wasn't hanging around again this time.

"What is it? Rose calm down. What is it?"

"He's there, he's back in the park again."

"Who? What are you talking about?"

"The old man, the one who killed Emily." She said while grabbing her father's hand and pulling him to the front door.

"Come on now, Rose. We've been through this. There was no man there."

"Just come one."

She opened the door and they went outside. The park was empty.

"Right, that's enough of that now, Rose." Her father scorned. "I'll have no more of old men or ghosts!"

"But I saw him. He must have left when I came to get you."

"He was never there, Rose! I know that it's hard and you saw a horrible, horrible thing. But this is just your imagination. You need to accept that."

"I, I saw him," she muttered, almost a whisper.

"No, Rose. You didn't."

For the rest of the day Rose walked around in a complete daze.

A combination of tiredness, confusion and grief had taken its toll on her. When bedtime came, she was more than ready for it. She fell asleep almost as soon as her head hit the pillow.

"Rose."

She woke startled once again. Her face held a look of terror as she was eye to eye with Emily once again.

"It's the old man, Rose."

"Daddy!" She screamed.

"He wants to bring his daughter back, Rose." A ghostly whisper came from Emily's pale dead lips.

"Daddy! Mummy!" Rose screamed again. She ran to the door and paused for a second to look back at Emily.

"He wants to bring her back, Rose."

She ran to her parent's room and spent the night in there.

Much to the annoyance of her parents, Rose spent the following three nights in their room, until her father had finally said that enough was enough and he demanded she sleep back in her own room. Rose sat awake for the whole night, waiting for Emily to show up. She didn't.

She kept peeking through her curtains to look over to the park, waiting to see the old man. There was nothing.

Finally she had to accept that her parents were right. She had imagined the whole thing. She promised herself that she would never forget Emily, she would always be her best friend. But she couldn't spend her whole life dwelling on her death.

The park looked beautiful now; it was almost Christmas and snow had covered every inch of it. Rose and her friend Bekki had run over there to have a snowball fight. They laughed as they pelted each other with snowballs. Rose had climbed the slide and then made an avalanche by sliding down it. Bekki ran to the swings. She brushed the snow off and jumped on. Kicking her legs back and forth she called to Rose.

"Come on, you can see for miles when you get high. Everywhere is white."

Rose stared at the swing. Her friend's deathtrap.

"No, I'm good. I'll pass."

"Come on, Rose. It's so beautiful," Bekki shouted.

There is no man, and there is no ghost. Her father's voice rang in her head. She remembered that she had proved to herself there was nothing to be afraid of. It had all been her imagination. She brushed off the snow and climbed on.

Swinging back and forth, now laughing along with Bekki, Rose couldn't believe that she was too scared to get on these because of a ghost. She laughed again at the thought.

"Come on swing higher!" Bekki giggled.

"OK, OK." Rose laughed as well.

Their laughter was joined by that of a man's. Rose looked behind her to see that god awful grin. The old man was stood behind her swing. He began to push her.

"Get off me! Get off, get off!" Rose screamed.

"What's the matter, Rose?" Bekki looked shocked.

"It's him, it's the man. Get off!" Tears now streamed down Rose's face.

The man kept pushing until she was going higher and higher. Bekki scraped her feet along the floor until she came to a stop.

"Rose, what's wrong?"

"It's him! He's pushing me!"

Bekki couldn't see anyone.

"Just stop yourself and get off."

"I can't," Rose cried, "he won't let me. He won't let me stop."

The old man's laughter filled the park. Bekki ran behind Rose's swing and tried to grab it to help her stop. It came back too fast and knocked her to the ground.

"Rose, you need to slow down and get off. What's the matter?"

Rose's face was now ice cold with her tears.

"I can't, he keeps pushing me."

"Then jump off," Bekki shouted, thinking that Rose had lost her mind.

"Yes jump!" The old man shouted and laughed. Only Rose heard him.

"Jump!" Bekki called

"Jump!" the old man repeated.

"I can't," Rose sobbed.

Bekki ran to Rose's house to get help. She didn't know what the hell was going on, but she knew there was something wrong.

"Jump!" The old man laughed "Jump!"

Finally, with no other option left. Rose let go of the swings. Her body flew through the air.

"*Rose!*" her father screamed.

She was turned upside down and landed on her head.

"*Rose!*" he ran to her and scooped her up from the ground.

He carried her back to the house, Bekki followed. She didn't know what to do. Looking at Rose's lifeless body in her father's arms, Bekki started to cry herself.

"Is she dead?" She asked bluntly.

"No," Rose's father replied. "She's just knocked herself out."

"Dad, Daddy?" A mumble came from Rose's mouth.

"Oh, thank God!" her father cried "Thank God, yes. Yes, sweetheart it's me."

"What happened?" Rose asked.

"You've just had a fall and banged your head that's all. Don't worry sweetheart."

"Is she going to be OK?" Bekki asked apprehensively.

"Yes, she'll be fine, Bekki. Thank you. I'm going to take Rose to bed, are you OK to call your mother to come and collect you? I'll be back down in a second."

"Yes, I'll be fine. I hope you're OK, Rose."

"Thank you, Bekki. I promise she'll be fine."

Rose's father carried her upstairs. He stripped her off her wet clothes and put her pyjamas on her then he put in her bed and tucked her in tight.

"You just stay there and get warmed up, OK? You've given me a hell of a fright. Just lie down and get some rest. He kissed her on the forehead.

"OK, thank you." Rose mumbled.

Her father closed the bedroom door and went down the stairs to check Bekki was OK.

Rose climbed out of bed and went to the bedroom window. She looked across to the park. There stood next to the swings again was the old man. He smiled and waved to Rose. She smiled and waved back.

"Thank you, Daddy," She whispered.

THANK YOU FOR READING

Dear reader, if you have reached this point then hopefully you have enjoyed this book. Firstly, I would like to thank you for giving me a chance to entertain you with my stories. I know sometimes it is a leap of faith trying an author you have never heard of. Hopefully, as long as people want to read my stories, I can continue to put more out there.

If you did enjoy this story. Would you please consider rating it and leaving a review on sites such as Amazon, Goodreads or any other similar sites? Reviews really do have a huge impact in the self-publishing market. It is the biggest selling tool that we have. Anything you have to say, whether a positive review or some constructive criticism will always be taken on board and used to hopefully improve on future work. Thank you very much. It really does go a long way.

MORE INFORMATION

If you would like to see any information regarding my other books you can find details at http://lennonslair.blogspot.co.uk/
    Please also feel free to contact me on Facebook or Twitter I would love to hear your thoughts and feedback.

Printed in Great Britain
by Amazon